# PALM BEACH

# PALM BEACH

*A Novel*

CORNELIUS VANDERBILT JR.

M. EVANS
*Lanham • Boulder • New York • London*

Published by M. Evans
An imprint of The Rowman & Littlefield Publishing Group, Inc.
4501 Forbes Boulevard, Suite 200, Lanham, Maryland 20706
www.rowman.com

Unit A, Whitacre Mews, 26-34 Stannery Street, London SE11 4AB

Distributed by NATIONAL BOOK NETWORK


First paperback edition 2015



British Library Cataloguing in Publication Information Available

**Library of Congress Cataloging-in-Publication Data**

The hardback edition of this book was previously cataloged by the Library of Congress as follows:

Vanderbilt, Cornelius, 1898–
Palm Beach / Cornelius Vanderbilt, jr.
p. cm.
1. Palm Beach (Fla.)—Fiction. I. Title.
PZ3.V2824 Pal
31001722

ISBN: 978-1-59077-512-7 (pbk. : alk. paper)
ISBN: 978-1-59077-513-4 (electronic)

∞™ The paper used in this publication meets the minimum requirements of American National Standard for Information Sciences—Permanence of Paper for Printed Library Materials, ANSI/NISO Z39.48-1992.

Printed in the United States of America

*To*

*PALM BEACH*
*Queen of Winter Playgrounds . Where these T.B.M. and these W. K. W. give every little bum a grand.*

# *PALM BEACH*

# CHAPTER I

THE slim girl in the big overstuffed armchair stared fixedly out the window. It was a large window—everything in the suite was large—hung with rose-colored damask.

Through the plate glass—like a picture framed in pink damask—the girl looked out at Palm Beach. There it was spread out before her, just as they'd told her it would be. White sand, blue sea with a line of frothy breakers and twisted palm trees.

And here she was in a five room suite at The Breakers, with seven trunks full of Paris clothes—really grown-up, sophisticated clothes, nothing the least schoolgirlish about them.

"Mrs. Vincent Duke and her charming debutante daughter Marjorie are among the recent arrivals at The Breakers."

"I ought to be very happy," Marjorie thought, craning her neck to get another look at the blond young man going by in a bicycle wicker chair. It looked like Gene Tunney but she couldn't be sure. She had met so many people in the last ten days, and had had so many more pointed out to her, that they all looked alike. Maybe it wasn't Gene Tunney. It might be Allie Fitz-Hamon. He had the same broad shoulders and the same alert way of carrying his fair head. Anyway, he was good looking, whoever he was.

Marjorie got up and walked over to the writing table. There wasn't anything to do just now, so she might as well write to Mid Bennett, and tell her all about Palm Beach and coming out. Mid was six months younger than Marjorie and Mrs. Bennett wanted her to go to Vassar. She said there was plenty of time for Mid to think about husbands.

"But there is nothing more important to a girl's future than a husband," Marjorie's mother had said when she had told her. "And many perfectly charming men don't care for college girls. They know too much. They've lost their bloom."

Marjorie had imparted this information to Mid and Mid had carried it to her mother. Isabelle Bennett, a tall, painfully thin Englishwoman who cared nothing for society and all but slept on horseback, had just laughed. "Darling, you're just a baby. Miss Chaise's school is about the only place left in the States where the girls aren't worldly-wise flappers at seventeen. But, my dear child, you aren't any more fitted to pick a husband than you are to earn your own living. I'm not going to have your heart broken into bits if I can help it!" This was Isabelle Bennett's reply.

"I wish she'd break her neck to bits. She will, too, if she persists in steeplechasing and riding to hounds and such nonsense!" Marjorie's mother had said, on being relayed her answer. The answer had to be relayed because the Dukes and the Bennetts weren't in the same set. The girls had been inseparable for years at Miss Chaise's, and had been in school in Switzerland together for a year, and at the same convent in France, but the families never met. The Bennetts were of the old Knickerbocker aristocracy. The Dukes, alas, were not.

So the argument had ended there. Mid had gone to Del Monte with her mother after graduation and Marjorie had been whisked off to England. It was to have been a holiday for the Dukes. A motor trip through the British Isles, a cottage in Brittany, a grand shopping orgy in Paris. Father's secretary and a chauffeur, and a maid, and a car. But Father hadn't been able to leave business, so just Marjorie and her mother set forth and the trip wasn't a success.

In the first place there was nobody on the boat; of course it was crowded, but with the wrong kind of people. And then Mrs. Duke had succumbed to a heart attack and they had spent the entire summer, except for two or three delirious weeks buying clothes in Paris, going from one specialist and one "cure" to another.

It was dull for Marjorie. She hadn't been able to conceal her loneliness and disappointment. She kept thinking about Mid, out in California. Mid had met Prince George and danced with him, and gone swimming and picnicking with him, at Monterey and Santa Barbara. "You'll meet far more interesting men after you come out." Mrs. Duke had promised from her pillows. "Men who will be seriously interested in you—not playing with you, as the Prince is playing with Mildred. He may find her amusing, but he certainly will not marry her, even if the Bennetts do think they're American royalty!"

And so the long summer had come to an end at last, and there had been the shopping orgy, glorious exciting days, choosing, trying on, having fittings. Days with skin specialists, days with hairdressers, long arguments about whether to cut her hair, or leave it long.

In the end they had decided to leave it long, the dark, loosely waved ends curled into a frivolous knot at the nape of her neck. It brought out the nice shape of her head, emphasized her small, clear-cut features, gave dignity to her darling slender being.

On the whole Marjorie Duke was satisfied with her looks. Yet she would have preferred to be golden and glowing like the rather notorious Mrs. Harry Brown of Chicago who was supposed to be the prettiest woman at Palm Beach. Or sinuous and exotic like Shirley Swayne, the movie actress. But even her fastidious mother was pleased with Marjorie's clear pink and white skin, the sheen of her dark wavy hair and the beauty of her wide apart, deep blue eyes which with their fringe of dark lashes gave a certain Celtic delicacy to her frank almost childish little face.

The papers had called her "a beauty" when they wrote up the coming-out party—that party that Marjorie had dreamed about and looked forward to for so long.

"At least I looked nice," she thought, a little wistfully, remembering her filmy Paquin gown, her sweet old-fashioned bouquet of ivory rosebuds and gardenias, and the hordes of young men who had bowed, smiled and danced with her and said things about the music and the decorations, and the punch—for all the world like the boys in dancing school parties for the last seven years.

She addressed the envelope:

Miss Mildred Bennett,
S 1 El Mirasol,
Santa Barbara, California

"Dearest Mid:

"We are having a very gay time here in Palm Beach, and I wish you were here or that I was in Santa Barbara with you."

But that didn't sound very gay. Mid would think she wished she were in Santa Barbara.

She'd begin again.

The sheet of paper went into little bits, into the wastebasket. Another sheet came out. Marjorie bit the pen.

What to say? "Last night we went dancing at the Colony Club." The club was all right, but it wasn't terribly exciting. Mother had insisted on leaving early.

Marjorie bit her pen again. What if she weren't going to be a success? Everyone said nice things to her, but nobody seemed to be much interested in her really.

The men were all too old, or too young—just boys—and the girls were so different from Mid and the girls she'd known all her life at Miss Chaise's.

"Aren't they—rather common?" she had asked a little nervously, after her first dinner dance at the Embassy. "That Throckmarten girl was tight—really she was, Mother, and she kept laughing so loud, and wanting to pour champagne down Mr. Varney's neck. And Mrs. Varney went off with that South American who dances so wonderfully, and Mr. Varney made jokes about it and—"

Her mother had been angry. "My dear, *don't* be childish. Evelyn Throckmarten is the sensation of the season. Engaged already. I hope you do as well."

"But, Mother, you wouldn't want me to—"

"Marjorie, don't be *absurd*. *You're* not the type. Now please don't copy Evelyn. But don't disappoint me. I've counted on this season for years, and if you're going to turn out a recluse like your father—"

"Oh, no, Mother—"

"But you act so peculiarly. You've had every advantage. With all his faults, your father has been lavish. In spite of poor health I've done everything. Nobody, not even Evelyn Throckmarten, has better clothes or more opportunities than you have. But if all my plans for you are ruined by your stubbornness—"

"But, Mother, I *want* to have fun!"

The tears had come then. She hadn't been able to hold them back. They had rolled down her cheeks babyishly, and she couldn't find her handkerchief.

"Oh, what's the use? My whole life is thwarted!" Her mother had sobbed, bursting into tears herself, and groping her way to the chaise-longue. Annie, the maid, who Marjorie was sure listened at keyholes, had come rushing into the room with lavender smelling salts, making little clucking sounds in her throat. "Oh, my poor dear lady. One of her terrible, terrible sinking spells. Come, dear Mrs. Duke—lean on Annie."

Mrs. Duke had glanced gratefully at the obsequious maid and cast a look full of self-pity and reproach at her frightened daughter.

"No," she had said, "I feel too weak to be moved. Send for Dr. Sweetser. And, Annie, call the Swami. I think I shall see him later, also. He helps me to find peace. I need peace."

She closed her eyes.

That all had happened four hours ago. The doctor had come. So had the Swami, an oily skinned youth who wore European clothes and a white turban.

Between them they must have restored that "peace" Mrs. Duke was always searching for, for she had sent word by Annie that she was feeling a little better and for Marjorie's sake would try to rise in time to dress for the Varneys' dinner at the Everglades.

It was almost six now. The crowds on the beach were thinning. People were being wheeled home. Marjorie went back to the window again and watched. She had given up trying to write to Mid.

There was a box of caramels on the table. She began to eat them methodically, beginning with the chocolate ones with the white centers and ending with the plain maple ones on the bottom layer.

She thought of having a marron glacé mousse sent up, and some macaroons and possibly a ham sandwich and some sweet pickles. She was hungry and eating between meals never affected her appetite for dinner. But her mother was afraid she'd ruin her complexion with too many sweets. Sweets didn't affect her complexion at all, but there wasn't any way of convincing Mrs. Duke. She'd worry just the same, and have another heart attack, maybe.

With a faint sigh, Marjorie gave up the idea. No use making trouble, there was enough already.

It was, though she didn't know it, her first concession towards growing up.

She fished the last caramel from the now empty box, and dropped it into the pink brocaded waste basket. With the decision not to antagonize her mother, by having marrons glacés and ice cream sodas between meals, had come another thought. The thought that though it was unlikely that Mother knew best, it was unwise to appear to notice it.

All her well-intentioned pleas for Mother to take more exercise, and not sleep so much, had made trouble. School hygiene, then, was not to be brought into the home. Mother *wanted* to be delicate. All right, let her be it! Only don't let her know that you knew!

The first line of repression settled around Marjorie Duke's frank childish mouth. Her blue eyes darkened, narrowed ever so little.

There wasn't any way to get out of this; she was here at Palm Beach to have a gay time, and be photographed as "Marjorie Duke, charming, debutante daughter of Mr. and Mrs. Vincent Duke of New York." To get married too. That was the real thing—to get married!

Mrs. Bennett had said that was what girls came out for, to make the right sort of match. She didn't want Mid to do it until she was a little older and had seen a little more of life.

Perhaps it would have been better if Marjorie could have waited. She didn't think so at first, but maybe Mrs. Bennett was right. She knew a lot, Mrs. Bennett. She let you talk to her, and she talked to you, as though you were grown up. You couldn't talk to Mother. You couldn't even depend on her. Father was too busy . . . way off in New York. . . .

Marjorie struck a little pose—an imitation of one she had seen Shirley Swayne affect in the movies.

She'd stand alone. She'd be independent. She'd let Mother think she was running things, and really she'd run them for herself . . . do as Father said, give in on the little things, hold out on the big ones.

Marjorie's heart was pounding now. She saw herself giving up marrons glacés forever—well, at least until she was married—and making up for it by having her way in big things: not waiting for Mother to feel better, but going ahead, making herself popular, landing the catch of the season.

Already she saw herself in white satin and Grandmother Wynne's rose point veil walking up the aisle of St. John's, and Mid in apricot mousseline de soie, and the other girls in green . . . or was that too obvious, apricot and green?

Marjorie bit a pink fingernail and paused to consider. Then she laughed, a little ruefully. She'd forgotten the bridegroom. Who'd he be?

Somebody nice, and important. Prince George? Don't be absurd. He won't marry an American. Well, that Portuguese Prince she had met at the Poinciana was certainly looking for an American. And lord knows I'm a rich one! No, his hands are too cold and slimy. Couldn't stand him. Maybe the Browning boy . . . everybody was after him, but he seemed like such a baby, with his funny little curly hair, and half-open mouth. . . . Allie Fitz-Hamon. . . .

Marjorie let her mind dwell on the name lovingly. Now there was a man a girl could really love. But that was the trouble . . . too many did.

Shirley Swayne was one of them, but she was

married. Only her husband, the French prince or viscount or whatever he was, was in France. Maybe they were going to get a divorce and then Allie would marry her. . . .

"Marjorie, are you going to mope all afternoon? Don't you know that I want you to dress and look as attractive as possible for this evening?"

There was Mrs. Duke in the doorway. She was wearing a mauve chiffon dressing gown that took the last vestige of color from her mottled, grayish cheeks and pale protuberant eyes.

She leaned heavily on Annie's arm, and looked really ill.

"I'm not moping. I couldn't very well go out when I knew you were ill," Marjorie began rebelliously, but when her mother put a thin, clawlike hand on her heart and shivered as if from chill, she weakened. Maybe she was wrong. Maybe Mother was really sick!

"Oh, Mother, you *are* ill. . . . Palm Beach isn't good for you. Let's go back to New York. Let me wire Father—"

Mrs. Duke raised a thin white hand. "No, I won't think of it. I'm here for your sake, and here I'll stay. I shall manage." She cast another appealing, self-pitying look at her adoring Annie. "With

Swami to help me I shall get through the winter somehow. Go and dress, dear. Wear the pink chiffon."

"If you're sure you're well enough," Marjorie kissed the soft, faded cheek.

Then she went off to don her white lace. It occurred to her that Allie Fitz-Hamon would like her better in white. And Mother? Oh, well . . . Marjorie was managing her own campaign now. Mother would have to be talked into it.

## CHAPTER II

THE fingers of Ernestine—the first personal maid Marjorie had ever had—were deft and swift. She was a master of make-up. She could use a jug of cold cream, a half box of powder, and make it seem that you were wearing your birthday complexion. Hair she had dressed, after an hour's manipulation, looked careless and casual. You'd swear it grew that way.

So, as Marjorie emerged at last, in her white lace with Father's graduation pearls around her neck, she looked like the very model of a schoolgirl complexion ad. Young. Unstudied. Natural.

Mrs. Duke, faintly mauve under her layers of make-up, was being helped into her wrap by the worried Annie.

One look at Marjorie and she was satisfied. "You look very well in that dress, my dear. Your father thinks I'm extravagant—but what does a man know of such things? Yes, it suits you."

Marjorie drew a deep breath. She said nothing. She was learning that lots of the things you worry about never happen. Her mother didn't even remember she had told her to wear pink!

So they started, down the slow, old-fashioned elevator, into the huge, cool lobby. It was the thing Marjorie liked best about the hotel. It was so comfortable, with its big, squashy flowered chintz chairs, its velvety green carpets, its high white ceilings. And smiling black boys in green uniforms, always at hand to do your bidding.

Past the rocking chair brigade, dowagers with tiaras and wattled chins, bald men with paunches, a few eager young girls, gawky in their unaccustomed long skirts.

Godfrey, the family chauffeur, was waiting at the door, hot and moist in his maroon livery.

"He ought to have a summer uniform," Marjorie said.

Mrs. Duke ignored the remark. But a moment later she irritably straightened Marjorie's slipping wrap and told her she hoped she wouldn't turn out to be careless about her appearance, like her father.

Marjorie smothered her resentment. She'd have much preferred driving in a hired open car, but Mother would have the Minerva, hateful, hot thing, sent down, and they had to ride everywhere in it.

"The best people bring their own cars to Palm Beach. It's a tradition." So what could you say to that?

The big car swished through the hedged garden, out into the open street. White and romantic, the road stretched ahead, the moonlight turning its utilitarian crushed oyster shells to tinsel. It made the familiar golf course a place of mysterious beauty. Down Cocoanut Row they sped, the headlights illumining the shiny curved trunks of the tufted palms. You could imagine monkeys and brilliant parrakeets in the trees.

"It *is* lovely here. It's fairy-like at night," Marjorie said breathlessly.

"Very pretty," said her mother. "If Mrs. Brown—that terrible blond—tries to talk to you, snub her. I disapprove of her."

It took less than ten minutes to reach the dark marquise of the Everglades Club, where the tall doorman in red velvet mantle and Spanish hat, waited.

Cars and wheel chairs were depositing their precious human freight, and like all exclusive clubs, it seemed to be crowded to capacity, with hurrying, anxious-faced men and women.

"Hello, Miss Duke!"

Marjorie turned at the sound of the familiar voice. "Oh, hello, Mr. Gander! Are you coming in? How nice!"

The tall, sandy haired youth elbowed his way forward. "Fine! I'll come right along with you," he said, grinning engagingly.

Mrs. Duke stared. Marjorie presented him.

In the entrance hall he melted away with a "See you later, Marjorie."

Mrs. Duke looked after him with rising distaste. The maid hurried forward to take their things.

"My dear, who in the world is it?"

"You mean Mr. Gander, Mother?"

"Gander! Quite an appropriate name, I must say. Where did you meet him? I don't like his manner."

Marjorie laughed. She *had* liked his manner. It said many things that to-night she particularly wanted to hear. It said that she was young and pretty and altogether adorable. It said that he admired her, and wanted to know her better. She delayed her answer, while she took a last minute look in the mirror at her perfect little nose. "I *asked* you where you met him?" her mother repeated icily.

"Oh, he's a newspaper man. I met him through Mr. Huntington, at the Cosden's party."

"A newspaper man? My dear child, it's against the rules of the club. You—brought him in! Oh well—there's Mrs. Varney waiting."

Puffing slightly, Mrs. Varney, short, fat, and middle-aged, came forward to meet them. "So happy you could come, my dear," she wheezed. "Such a hot night. We're so lucky to have Lord Allan Fitz-Hamon. I hear he admires your charming daughter."

The Lawrences were there, tall, bald Henry, and short, plump Mazie-Beth. Mazie-Beth was a bride of little more than a year, but she looked old and bored with life, not the least like the debutante photographs Marjorie remembered seeing in Vanity Fair and Vogue when she was in school.

Henry looked hot, and rather disheveled. "The hotel valet made a frightful job of my tail coat," he was saying, trying to look over his shoulder at the tails. "I really had forgotten one has to wear the things here. I should have gotten a new one—"

"Men don't wear them in California," his wife cut in.

"Now, Mazie-Beth, don't let's talk about California."

"Well, it's really a lot nicer than Palm Beach. We have cool nights—"

"Here come Lord Allan and John Browning. I'm sure you all know each other. Shall we go into dinner now?"

Browning, out of breath, looking anxiously at his hostess. "I suppose I'm late," he began, a little ungraciously. "I killed my red bug—"

Mrs. Duke raised her lorgnette.

"My red bug! You know, my little scooter, it goes with a motor. Yes, the mixture was wrong. I was scooting along the lake trail and it died. Just died. I had to get a dinge and a chair. Gee, I hope no one swipes my red bug."

Idiot, Marjorie thought. He may be the catch of the season, but I'd die if I had to listen to him and his red bug all day long. But Allie . . .

And there was Allie, correct to the last ribbon of his decorations. Oh, he was nice. Everything about him was nice. His low, well modulated English voice. His smooth fair hair, his tiny waxed mustache.

And no Shirley Swayne!

Little thrills of excitement chased down Marjorie's spine. Palm Beach was looking up. She gave a warm hand to Allie . . . smiled up at him delightedly.

"Now the evening is going to be perfect!"

Marjorie laughed again. It was so easy to laugh to-night. She caught her mother's eyes. Her mother was satisfied.

They were dining in the patio that overlooked the lagoon. Waiters in dark velvet breeches and brilliant sashes brought exotic dish after dish.

Silent, speeding launches deposited belated guests from luxurious houseboats lying in Lake Worth beyond. Gondolas glided smoothly over the waters. Out in the lagoon somewhere a gondolier was singing; snatches from *Negra* came softly over the water to them.

"I'd love to be in a gondola," Marjorie sighed.

"Then we'll go after dinner. It's too hot to dance," Allie said.

She turned to see fat, elderly John Huntington standing by her side. "Well, well, how's everything? Mazie-Beth, lovely as ever, and little Marjorie! Mrs. Varney and Mrs. Duke looking younger every day . . . the Palm Beach climate—that's what it does."

The men were rising—young Browning reluctantly, and with a scowl. Marjorie beamed. "Hello!" she said to Erskine Gander, at Huntington's elbow.

"Call me Goose!" he replied, laughing.

"Perfect!" Browning sneered.

"How about a little dance," Huntington cut in, before Browning could finish.

"Oh, not to-night, Josh. The humidity—"

Not in the least disconcerted, he bowed graciously toward Mrs. Duke. "Too much humidity for you too?"

To Marjorie's surprise her mother rose, smiling pleasantly.

When they had gone on toward the music, the others turned to watch the dancers, the brilliant play of lights, the pastel-colored gowns.

Young Browning turned toward Marjorie, but before he could speak Gander was taking her arm, and they were following the older couple.

Marjorie heard Mrs. Varney, always the perfect hostess, slide graciously into the breach. She wanted to laugh. It served Browning right. He was too officious. And it would show Allie that she had admirers—lots of them.

"Of course I did an awful thing," Gander was

saying in her ear. "I had no business here; they keep newspaper men out, do you know that? But I had to get in—I'm after a story, so I just barged in with you? Forgive me?"

She laughed. They danced, young, happy, in tune with the wild Spanish music.

"Where's the beautiful Miss Swayne?" he asked, breaking the spell.

"I'm sure I don't know," she answered a bit stiffly, and in spite of herself, a faint blush spread itself over her cheek, crept down to her neck.

The newspaper man smiled to himself. So that's it? She likes the fellow herself. Well! Well!

She felt a tap on her shoulder. Browning, darn him. Browning was cutting in!

There was no help for it. She had to dance with him.

He wasted no time. "That fellow certainly lives up to his name," he said, "coming in here with a tux. Who is he anyway?"

"He comes from Seattle. His father is one of the richest men in the northwest. Didn't you ever hear of the Gander pulp mills?"

"No, I never did. And the Ganders never heard of coat tails, I gather."

"Oh, Brownie, don't be nasty!"

"I'm not nasty. I don't like the fellow. Looks like a bounder to me. I suppose he told you all about his father and his dough—"

"No—Josh Huntington did."

"That old reprobate. Know what he does? He gets a commission for bringing the Follies down here every winter. And I shouldn't doubt if he got something for introducing people. Lots of people say he does—"

Marjorie just laughed. "Brownie, you're incorrigible." And she was really thinking: "You big, round-eyed, curly-headed baby. Even if he does I'd rather dance with Huntington than you!"

It was a relief when the music stopped and they could go back to the table. The waiter who looked like a toreador brought Baked Alaska, and café noir.

"What is this?" Gander wanted to know. He and Josh had drawn up chairs and joined the party.

"What, you from Seattle, don't know Baked Alaska?" Browning interposed.

"It's ice cream and meringue. They bake it in the oven," the literal hostess explained.

"They serve the café noir with it so you won't mistake it for the fish course," Josh Huntington volunteered.

He was in fine form. Couldn't wait to get everyone out in gondolas. Marjorie held back, expectant, eyes on Allie, fearful that they'd be separated.

She needn't have worried. Josh Huntington had everything arranged. "Marjorie and Allie and Goose in this one and Mrs. Duke—"

"Oh, but Mother was so ill this afternoon. I wonder if she ought—"

"I feel entirely well," Mrs. Duke said, glaring stonily at Marjorie.

"In case she feels indisposed, I have a little something I always carry with me," Josh grinned. "So Mrs. Duke had better go in my boat. And Henry Lawrence. Mrs. Duke will want to hear about Henry's Zorns—he's got more fat women in his house than the Sultan of Turkey."

Out in the lagoon they slid noiselessly through deep rushes, rising black and sinister from the waters. Myriad flecks of light, phosphorescence of southern waters, followed the gondolier's pole. Little twinklings, reflections from portholes of distant yachts, bobbed like fireflies in the water. The moon left a path of silver as it moved on its endless journey through the sky.

"It's like a night in Egypt," Allie said, and Marjorie thrilled at the touch of his shoulder next to hers.

"I'd love to see Egypt. . . ."

"I'll take you. When shall we start?"

"We can start any time, can't we, Marj?" Gander put in, laughing. "I'll go along, Fitz, as your guide and chaperon, can't I, Marjorie?"

"Chaperon! Who wants a chaperon—"

"Are you proposing to me?"

"Not here—it's too public," Allie laughed. "Wait till we land, won't you?"

Marjorie was glowing with life and laughter. Allie was making love to her, he really was, and Gander liked her too. While she was searching for something bright and sparkling to say, the moment passed. The other gondola drew close alongside.

"But I had the worst time of all getting the Swan," Henry Lawrence's dull voice was droning. "I had an offer from that kike—what's his name—Michaels, not Michaels—Levy—"

"How interesting," Mrs. Duke moaned on.

"Home, James!" Huntington directed, pinching the gondolier's calf. His patience also was exhausted.

So the other gondola had to follow.

Browning was waiting on the float. He looked

belligerent, and even to Marjorie's unpracticed eye, it was apparent that he had been drinking.

"I hear you're a newspaper man," he shrilled at Gander. "Is it true? I want to know if it's true. I'm asking you? Are you going to answer?"

"Yes, it's true. What of it?"

"Then how did you get in here? What business a newspaper man coming in gentleman's club? Too damn many press agents 'round here. Ruining Palm Beach."

"Steady there, Browning. You'll have the load overboard!" Josh called from the next gondola. "Let go the gondola. Here you, gondolier, push off!"

But it was too late. Browning already had hold of Gander's coat. "I'm waiting for my answer!"

"Let go, you fool!" Allie commanded. "You'll tip us over."

"I'm just asking a civil question. I'm waiting for my answer!"

Marjorie felt her mother's eyes upon her. It was all Browning's fault, but she'd get the blame.

With a sudden, lithe spring, Gander leaped to the landing. "We'll talk this over later," he said. "You're starting a row. Do you want to embarrass Miss Duke?"

"I want to know how you got in?" Browning drunkenly insisted.

Gander turned to assist Marjorie, who was stepping from the gondola. A blow from Browning's fist nearly floored him.

Marjorie held her breath. If there was a fight her mother would never forgive her. Servants were hurrying. People were rising from their chairs in the dining room.

Allie sprang to the float. "I'll settle this," he said, and oh how Marjorie loved the sound of his calm, unruffled British voice.

## CHAPTER III

ALLAN FITZ-HAMON took the boy by the shoulders. In his strong hands the spindly heir to the Browning millions was helpless as a reed in the wind.

"He's my guest," he said. "If you have any objections you may take it up with the Board. But this is neither the time nor the place. Pull yourself together, lad. You're making a scene. Come with me—we'll talk it over—"

His arm around Browning, he half led, half dragged him away, motioning with his free hand for Gander to stay back.

"Dear Lord Fitz-Hamon—" Mrs. Duke murmured, feeling faint after her fright.

"Good old Allie—"

"He saved a nasty situation—"

People had returned to dinner and dancing, waiters turned away. It was nothing after all. Just young John Browning who had had a drop too much.

Fitz-Hamon returned for the dancing. The

newspaper man thanked him, a little awkwardly, Marjorie thought. "It was nothing," Allie said. "The boy was tight. Overlook it, will you, Gander?"

In the dressing room, later, Marjorie, reddening her lips, waited for her mother's verdict.

It wasn't long coming.

"I don't want you to be seen with that Goose person again, Marjorie. It was very embarrassing. Poor Alfreda Varney! And wasn't Lord Fitz-Hamon wonderful? The English know how to do things. He admires you, dear. By the way, we're driving him home. Or rather, to Bradley's—there's a man he has to see."

In the big car, the Dukes, mother and daughter, and Lord Allan Fitz-Hamon sank into the back seat.

Allie didn't say a word to Marjorie. Mrs. Duke did all the talking. . . .

"And how is your sister Princess Carolyn? Such a beautiful girl. We met her at Monte Carlo . . . well, it must have been four years ago—no, five. It was the year we had Marjorie in the convent. . . . Mr. Duke? He's well, thank you. The stock market, you know. No, the flurry didn't bother him. . . . How is your uncle, the Earl? Your uncle is an earl, isn't he? Americans do get those things mixed. . . . Yes, of course . . . Earl of Raleigh, I've seen his portrait, and his sisters the Ladies Victoria Maria and Sophronia Isabella?"

Marjorie's color rose. Mother was asking too many questions. Fitz-Hamon would see what she was getting at. . . .

"Good night, Marjorie." They had stopped at Bradley's, and Allie was getting out. The words weren't anything. It was the way he said them. They were a caress, a promise, a secret bond between them.

"My word! What's that?" he cried suddenly, before she could answer.

Marjorie followed his pointing finger, and couldn't suppress a giggle. His easy laugh rang out. "Disgraceful!" Mrs. Duke quavered, raising her lorgnette to get a better view.

A young man in coat tails and battered opera hat was pushing a grinning colored boy in a chair. No mistaking him—it was Brownie, very, very tight.

"I'll look after him in a bit," Fitz-Hamon said laughing. "Perhaps I can persuade him to let the boy push *him* home."

"You're too good to him," Mrs. Duke said

warmly, and when they left him she said, "There's the man for you, Marjorie. My mind's made up."

Marjorie was silent. She looked down at her hands, and half shook her head.

"What? You aren't interested? Now, Marjorie, if you're going to make trouble for me—after all my plans—"

"It's not I. It might be Lord Fitz-Hamon. Isn't he entitled to an opinion?" she asked wearily.

For the wheel chair episode hadn't taken all her attention. She had seen the blue Minerva, so much like their own car, driving in to Bradley's. She knew the car. Shirley Swayne's. And she had a glimpse of the exotic Shirley, great pearls in her ears, cloth of silver over her white shoulders, ready to get out at Bradley's.

"That's the 'man' he was going to meet there. Shirley Swayne," she thought, bitterly.

Her mother babbled on the rest of the way home. Marjorie sat motionless, gazing at nothing, out the window. Allie Fitz-Hamon wasn't through with Shirley Swayne. Anyway, how could she, a lady, hope to compete with a seasoned coquette like the Swayne woman? And the Browning boy was out. Cad—no other name for it. She wouldn't marry him—not if she had to be left over for seven seasons, not Marjorie.

"I won't sleep a wink," Marjorie decided, sipping the hot chocolate she had had sent up to console her, and adding ladle after ladle of whipped cream.

But she was asleep almost as soon as her curly head touched the pillow, and it was the telephone, almost nine hours later, that woke her.

"Good morning!"

Allie's voice! She was wide awake in a moment.

The Beach and Cycle Club—for a swim and lunch? She'd love it. Yes, in half an hour!

She was too excited for breakfast, and besides there wasn't time. She had to be just right. Shirley Swayne might be more thrilling at night, but there was one time when it paid to be young—in the morning!

The Beach and Cycle Club had its own isolated beach. Under gayly striped umbrellas, in colorful lounging pajamas, Palm Beach's inner circle disports itself around noon every day.

They lay on the sand, Marjorie in her canary-colored low backed swimming suit, Allie close beside her. So they both saw Josh at once. Josh—all two hundred pounds of him, swathed in a light blue lounging suit.

"My God," Allie groaned, "here comes that pest. Pretend you don't see him."

"Oh, poor Josh," said Marjorie, too happy to snub anyone, even the loud-mouthed Josh.

But it wouldn't have made any difference—Josh had seen them.

"Ah, two more swells near the ocean swell!" Josh shouted. "May I make a third?" Making himself comfortable, close to Marjorie.

From the other direction, Madge Olsen, the fashion writer, hailed Fitz-Hamon, "You're wanted on the telephone, Allie. They say it's the Poinciana but I'm sure it's one of your women!"

"Thanks," Allie laughed. Marjorie laughed too, but not as heartily.

"That Olsen woman is a cat," Josh ventured kindly.

Marjorie's heart warmed to him.

"Are you having a good time, child?" he asked, watching Allie's bronzed legs stepping over prone social registerites.

"Oh, wonderful!" Her eyes were on Allie too.

"Do you know everybody? How long have you been here?"

"Long enough to meet millions—but there are still millions left."

"Well—there's Nasty Condé—the nice stubby, plump boy over there; he's the publisher of *Oblivion,* you know. He's with Mrs. Belmont Tiffany—that large baby who's drugstored her complexion. Hoytie Wiborg is the one with the slivvery pajamas; she's engaged again—an apple seller, I think, this time. With her? That's Barbara Post—once a Loew, but now in high. They call her husband the Black Swan—the good looking chap beside the Jumbo Squab. And he who lisps and twitters is Frankie Crowingshield with his boy friend Charlie Towne. . . . Now what else can I tell you? How do you like this little old penínsúla anyway?"

Joining in his mood, Marjorie laughed. "But I thought it was an island."

"Don't you know any joggraphy?"

"I didn't come here to study geography."

"Physiographies?"

Marjorie forgot the play. Her watchful eye caught sight of Allie, coming back, but oh, so slowly. Allie knew everybody and everybody knew him. He had to stop to talk to Vincent Astor. Then Bernie Gimbel. Then Otto Kahn.

"If you go around with Allie you'll soon know Palm Beach," Josh said grinning.

"I thought it was the girls Allie knew! It's the men I want to meet." Marjorie couldn't help it—the words just slipped out.

"You can't be in Burke's peerage without knowing both. . . . Ah, here he comes now."

"How about lunch? Aren't you hungry?" Allie asked. Marjorie felt a little sorry for Josh, until he said, not the least abashed,

"Well, I guess I'll go put the nose bag on too!"

"Terrible bore," Allie muttered, as they went up to the coral reef where lunch was to be served. "Butts in on everybody."

It was hard to talk above the music. Allie looked, rather than said the things that Marjorie ached for him to say.

"Who was she?" she asked at last.

"Who?"

"The girl who called you on the telephone?"

"It wasn't a girl. It was my broker. You're not jealous of him, are you?"

"Of course not!" But the sun was brighter, the music was sweeter and Allie made it Paradise when he begged her to have tea and dance later that afternoon at the Cocoanut Grove.

It was over all too soon, even with the promise of dancing at the Cocoanut Grove, to make the parting easier. It had been such a gorgeous morning. Like the ones she had dreamed about.

Dozens of camera men had taken her pictures with Allie on the beach.

"Don't be a silly, Marjorie Duke," she told herself sternly in the hotel that afternoon. "It doesn't mean a thing!"

But she was sure that it did mean something. Her picture with his would be in the Eastern papers, in Vogue, Vanity Fair. She hadn't been too eager—she knew enough to seem reluctant, but she had turned her best profile, looked unconscious of what was going on, and as charming as she could, just as all camera-shy people are supposed to look.

There was just one fly in the ointment. The afternoon papers had the news that Shirley Swayne's husband, Vicomte Henri de L'Inois, was in Paris getting a divorce on the grounds of desertion.

So Shirley would be free and—trust Shirley—without a breath of scandal. No reason why Allie couldn't marry her if he wanted to. He probably would.

In the hour of her dressing for Cocoanut Grove Marjorie gave up Allie a dozen times. No use letting herself care too much, and then seeing him marry the movie actress. Yes, but why give up without a struggle? Wouldn't a man in Allie's position—everyone knew he was poor—want to marry a real heiress, rather than a glamorous star with a pseudo title and just enough to make a show? Yes, but who wants to be married for money? Allie wouldn't really marry anyone for money. His first wife had been a Follies Girl without a cent.

She let herself think about the man himself. The long, lean brownness of him. The beauty of his thin, aquiline features. His instinctive good taste. Oh, to go through life with someone like that! To be away from Mother. . . .

That thought shocked her a little. To think that she wanted to get away from her mother. And for years she had been wanting to be with her. All those years at school, looking forward to coming out, and going places with her mother . . . no use counting on Father, he wouldn't leave business.

She'd always wanted to be in love, too, and now that she was, she was unhappy.

She put her head down on the dressing table, and shut her eyes.

"Tired, Miss Marjorie? Will you dress now? Or had I better notify Lord Allan—"

"No, I'll dress," Marjorie said, and gave herself into the hands of Ernestine.

Twenty minutes later, in printed chiffon and a huge, flattering black straw hat, she was in a chair with Allie, laughing, vivacious, carefree as a debutante is supposed to be.

Cocoanut Grove is just within the labyrinth of jungled garden which separates the Royal Poinciana from a gaping world. It lies midway between the hotel and the old Flagler residence, the first mansion erected in Palm Beach, surrounded now by a veritable fairyland of palatial estates.

At teatime it is the vortex of gayety and smartness. Here at little marble topped iron tables, under the palms, sit the rich, the powerful, the fashionable, the distinguished. Here you will see Tony Biddle, the Countess Bracatti, Peggy Joyce, turbulent Dudley Field Malone, the immaculate William Rhinelander Stewart, Nancy Harriman, Bill Rockefeller, Princess Bibesco, the haughty Baroness de Cartier de Marchienne, George Cohan, the impeccable Jimmy Walker, Flo Ziegfeld, Maria Jeritza, Helen Morgan, Roy Howard, titian-haired Helen Fahnstock, Elsie de Wolfe, his Excellency the Persian Minister.

And anyone else who has the price of admission!

The usual heavy-jowled, gray-suited gentleman lolled just without the enclosure—the hotel dick.

He was talking with Erskine Gander.

Josh Huntington entered with the notorious Mrs. Harry Brown, radiantly beautiful, seductively golden, in her diaphanous chiffons.

"There's Mrs. Jerome Bonaparte," Josh was saying. "You know she's the Strebeigh girl from points West. Now she's all Napoleon."

"He's the original wise-cracker," Gander smiled, as Josh passed.

"And the original gold-digger on his arm. Have you any dope on her?"

"No—why?"

"I have a tip from headquarters. She plays every capital. We're trying to find out who she gangs with. Watch old Josh fall for the smirk. That's going to cost him plenty!"

The music had begun again. Under the palms

the guests were dancing. Gander's eyes found Marjorie, followed her as she danced with Allie round the floor.

"There's the one that puzzles me. Allie Fitz-Hamon. Seems like a nice fellow, but I feel funny about him. He affects me as a cat does some people—"

"Yeh? I heard you liked the little Duke girl—"

"Who, me? No—that isn't it—cute kid, though. No, what I mean is I've seen that Fitz-Hamon face some place, and I'm trying to place it. I've got a funny feeling about him, I tell you."

The detective grinned. "You better stick to your scandal sheet and leave the detective work to me," he advised good-naturedly. "Fitz-Hamon's all right."

A waiter was making his way to Fitz-Hamon's table. Fitz-Hamon followed him into the hotel.

"That guy gets more telephone messages than Brigham Young did in his prime. Now the lady is left all to her lonesome," the detective observed, with a sly wink for Gander.

Gander winked back. Then with an exaggerated imitation of his friend the dick's flat footed shuffle he moved toward the entrance.

In a moment he was with Marjorie.

She wasn't too glad to see him. "May I sit down with you for a moment?" he begged. "I've just got to talk to you. I can't begin to tell you how sorry I am for all the trouble I caused. I had no business in the place the other night, but I just had to get in, and I had no idea how things would turn out. Now I'll never forgive myself. And it was darn nice of Fitz-Hamon to come to the rescue the way he did."

Instantly Marjorie was all animation. "It was rather wonderful," she said. "He—he's about the most wonderful person I've ever known. . . . But I suppose I haven't met many people."

He saw she wanted to talk. "It's a great thing to meet someone who you feel understands, and speaks your language," he said seriously. "And do you know, that's the way I feel about you—sort of as though you were a kind of kid sister—" he added hastily, noting the troubled gleam in her expressive eyes.

"Oh, do you really? Oh it would be nice to have a brother. I haven't one, you know. I'm an only child, and my chum is way off in California. She's going to go to college. I'm kind of lonely . . . but of course I'm having a wonderful time!"

"Oh, of course! Everybody knows that—"

"I mean, I hope I'm going to be a success and all that. But Allie Fitz-Hamon is wonderful, isn't he? Oh, do you know Shirley Swayne? She's getting a divorce—isn't she?"

"Yes, but I don't believe there's anything between her and Fitz . . . that's what you mean, isn't it?"

She dropped her eyes. "I wondered—"

"Sure. That's natural. Lots of people wonder. When you like a person you wonder a lot about them. I tell you—if I find out, I'll tell you, but I don't think there's anything in it. Some of the scandal sheets print anything they can get regardless of how much trouble it starts."

"But aren't you on a scandal sheet?" she smiled.

"The New York Press! Oh, my God! The Press a scandal sheet? Why it's one of the most dignified papers in the country. I'm down here to get news. I get interviews with visiting celebrities, I put the Palm Beach news on the wire for several of the big eastern papers."

He was so genuinely upset that Marjorie laughed out loud. He was so friendly and frank and boyish.

The music had begun again. It was a dreamy waltz, and Marjorie saw the rotund Josh Huntington on his way to their table. She was just going to ask Gander to dance with her, to escape Josh, when he gained the table, and horror on horrors, he had with him the blond Mrs. Harry Brown.

"So you've left Burke's Peerage for the Fourth Estate," he bellowed good-humoredly. "You know Mrs. Brown, Marjorie, don't you? She and Goose are old friends!"

The blond gushed, Marjorie acknowledged the introduction coolly . . . so Goose knew her too!

Before she could say another word Josh had her firmly by the arm. "Shake a leg with grandpa before this waltz ends. I don't know why they don't have more waltzes. Too many lousy foxtrots. Give me a good old-fashioned whirl like this!"

When Allie returned his table was empty. Josh and Marjorie were dancing, and Goose had the blond Mrs. Brown on the floor.

He had not long to wait though, and the whole party arrived at once.

"Allie himself, not a moving picture! I've been trying to see you for days. Don't you ever answer the phone?" Mrs. Brown cried.

Allie, too . . . did all Palm Beach know Mrs. Brown?

"Waiter, bring another chair!" The vivacious Ivy Brown called. "You don't mind if I sit next to

Allie, do you, Miss Duke? We're such old friends . . . way back in England. Come on, sit down, Josh—come on, Goose, we can always use an extra man!"

Allie's good humor had left him. Marjorie was afraid he would insult Josh—that is, if anything could insult Josh. She began to look around anxiously. It would be just like her mother to come to have a look at her and Allie having a solitary tea together, and find her with the Brown woman and Goose instead.

"Aren't you going to spike the tea?" Ivy's shrill voice penetrated Marjorie's thoughts.

Allie murmured something.

"You must have got religion!" Ivy snorted. "That's what comes of having so many churches. Never saw so many churches as there are in Palm Beach in all my life. The town is full of them. Well, give me plenty of sugar if I can't have it spiked. I've got to have something to take the taste out—"

Allie was beginning to make ineffectual attempts to signal the waiter. Finally he called in a loud voice, "*L'addition!*"

On the way home in the chair they tried to

regain the lost feeling of intimacy that had been theirs in the morning, but it was gone.

Marjorie left him reluctantly. Childishly she thought that if they stayed together a little while longer it might come back. But Allie hurried off, and to make things worse Josh Huntington was in the lobby—waiting for her.

"See here, child—I want to talk to you," he began right away. "I know you were offended because I brought Ivy to the table. You just can't afford to be that way in Palm Beach. Let grandpa tell you. This isn't Newport.

"It was once upon a time, but it isn't now. You've got to be in the social register—right down in black and white—before you can crash Bailey's Beach or the Casino. Here any mongrel with money can get by anywhere, and if you want to be ritzy this is not the place to be it. You just enjoy the palm trees and the climate, and take the Ivy Browns the way you would mosquitoes. Anyway, Ivy's all right. Damn fine looking girl. Used to be in the Scandals. Married to some old ham and egg —nobody ever sees him. And if you ever get in a jam—"

"Which I trust I won't—"

"We'll hope not, child. But if ever you do, Ivy

is the girl to get you out. She's got something on everybody in Who's Who."

Marjorie made a move to go, but old Josh piloted her over to one of the squashy chairs. "Some more things I want to tell you," he continued.

"Don't get so wrought up over Allie's girls. Everybody has girls. Even I have. Doesn't mean a thing. Fellow like that makes a lot better husband than a sap like young Browning. Understands women, knows how to treat them. Now do you feel better?"

Marjorie did. She almost liked Josh Huntington. After all, he knew what he was talking about. He was a man of the world.

And when she reached her room and found a long box of deep red roses, and Allie's card—"Lord Allan Drackett Fitz-Hamon" and the one little line, "Am I never to see you alone?—Allie" the disappointment of the afternoon was almost forgotten.

Mrs. Duke, spending the day in bed, fretfully dismissed the Swedish masseuse and called Marjorie into her room.

"A beautiful card from Lord Allan," she said. "I knew he admired you. Now if you don't do anything stupid—"

"Oh, Mother, you opened my flowers!"

"Don't be absurd. Go and dress. We're going out with the Lawrences."

"Are we going to the Colony to-night?"—That was one of Allie's favorite haunts—maybe she'd see him. "I'll wear Allie's roses—"

After all, it was a nice world. Marjorie whistled in her bath. Her mother was probably right. Allie did admire her or he wouldn't have sent the roses and that message. She began to plan a little speech that she would make to him that night.

## CHAPTER IV

THE Lawrences called for them at eight.

From the start everything was wrong. Henry, in his coat-tails, still unpressed, wanted to ride in front with the chauffeur.

"I don't want to crowd you ladies," he said.

"You mean you want to ride out in the air!" Mazie-Beth shrilled. "But no you don't, Henry Lawrence. You can stand it if I can. It was your idea to come to Palm Beach, not mine. I'd have stayed right in California with my mother if you hadn't—"

"Oh, Mazie-Beth, for God's sake! Now let me think. Wait, driver. Where did I tell you? What hotel was that, Mazie-Beth?"

"Maybe it was the Colony," Marjorie put in hopefully.

"That's it—that's it—the Dannelli—the Dannelli, driver!"

There was no music at dinner. "This isn't the place I meant," Henry said. "It was the Alba I wanted. No, not the Alba. Oh well, this is all right."

And after the seven courses were over, and they were ready to drive off Henry caught sight of the Colony spelled in red Neon lights. "There," he said, with the air of one who has been cheated. "That's where I wanted to come!"

"That's what I told you!" Marjorie couldn't keep it back. The thought of Allie, dancing with someone else, perhaps looking for her inside, was just too much.

"Oh, did you? Thought you said Dannelli. Beastly names in this place. Let's go and see the Seminole Indians. Over at West Palm Beach. We're lucky. They're only here for a week every year and this is just the time."

"Very interesting," Mrs. Duke murmured. She hadn't the least idea what Henry had said.

In the car Mazie-Beth turned to Marjorie. "Do you hear him? Rambling on about Indians. Yesterday it was etchings. To-morrow it will be first editions, all mildew. Don't ever marry a dilettante. Marry a business man like your father. Then you can live anywhere you like. I would like to live at home. But just because Henry has no work he has to move all the time. Some day he'll be dead, and they'll arrest me for killing him and they'll be right. . . . Listen to him now—"

They were crossing the yellow wooden bridge to West Palm Beach. Lights glowed from the windows of many tall buildings in the commercial city across the bay.

"That's a beautiful sight," Henry was saying. "The artist could paint the picture, the builder could lay the bricks, but the masterpiece would be what the poet would say of the reflections."

"He'll go on like that for hours," Mazie-Beth stormed.

Marjorie stifled a giggle.

Henry went right on, "I wonder if the architect who designed those buildings ever thought of the symmetry of those windows in the daytime and their absolute entanglement by night. Scattered harebrained crew! They make me think of soldiers in ragged formation in Soviet Russia by night—"

"Have you tried that new orange blossom cream? They make it in Los Angeles—" Mazie-Beth's voice rose above her husband's.

Henry had begun on the Indians. "We still have the primitive races here. These Seminoles come in from the Everglades for this one week every year. They live on sofka—"

"It makes me think of vodka . . . that Russian drink," Mrs. Duke mumbled.

"No, it's a food," said the careful Henry. "It's made from the heart of palms. The Seminoles' dress is also peculiar. The men are garbed like women, in burlap, with bright horizontal stripes—"

"Where do they get the burlap?"

"I must look that up. Ah, here we are. You'll soon see. Go on, driver, we must find the Indians. Well, ask where they are. What's that? Shoot!"

For the Indians were no longer there. Their week was up and once more they were in the Everglades.

"Well, what shall we do now?" Mazie-Beth wanted to know. "Now that we've done our duty by the Indians maybe we can have some fun. If this was Del Monte we could go to Canary Cottage."

"We could go to Bradley's, but we've got little Marjorie with us."

"Don't be silly, Henry. She's past eighteen!"

"Is it all right, Mrs. Duke?"

Of course Mrs. Duke agreed, so they started back to Bradley's. Marjorie didn't care much. The evening was ruined anyway, and Allie would never see his roses, wilting already, pinned to her shoulder.

In all the milling mob of black coated men and white-shouldered women, Allie was the first one to catch Marjorie's eye, however. He bowed, and went on with his game.

Mrs. Duke raised her lorgnette, "Isn't that Lord Allan? Is he gambling?"

"That's what they come here for," Henry tacitly explained.

Allie was at the roulette wheel, plunging on the odd numbers, 5, 7, 9, 11. He seemed to be winning. The croupier's little rake was diverting wobbly piles of blue chips towards Allie's elbow.

"Hello there!"

It was the inevitable Josh, playing at the next table. He too seemed to be winning. "I'm lousy with money. Ivy, here, has brought me luck."

"Poison Ivy," Mrs. Duke murmured under her breath. She began to think about leaving. If Mrs. Harry Brown of Chicago was here, she had no interest in remaining. But Henry had already disappeared. He was standing behind a fat dowager in black jet, industriously working out a mathematical system.

Unwilling to seem too interested in Allie, Marjorie went and stood near Josh. She stood directly behind a short, thickset man, with a crafty, piggish face.

"Atta boy," Ivy shouted, every time the croupier's rake pushed the chips Josh's way.

And then a queer thing happened.

"I beg your pardon," the pig-faced man interposed quietly, "That was my pile, sir. I'll thank you to return it to me!"

Josh drew back, his face flaming. "Why—why—" he sputtered. "I thought—I could swear I placed mine right there on the line. Are you sure—"

"Be a sport, Josh!" Ivy had her arm on Josh's. "The fellow's right. It's his winning."

"But it was Josh's!" Marjorie cried involuntarily. "I saw him put it down myself."

"Well, that's what I thought! I am sure I put it there."

"There must be no argument at the table, gentlemen." The croupier's voice was like a knife.

"I tell you it's the man's—let him have his winning, Josh," Ivy said coldly, and then turning her blond beauty full on the abashed Marjorie she said, "You don't understand the game, I'm sure. I'm an old-timer. I saw the play. Pay up, Josh."

Josh paid.

Allie had left his table. He was supporting Mrs.

Duke. "I think your mother is feeling faint—" He was signalling Marjorie.

And at that moment Mrs. Duke crumpled, and nearly fell. Allie helped to carry her out, and it took Mazie-Beth and Marjorie, and two maids, to revive her.

"Oh, Marjorie, why did you interfere?" she moaned. "What will your father say?"

Josh also had left his table. "Don't worry, Marjorie, I'll get Goose to hush this up—"

"Hush it up?"

"Keep it out of the papers!"

"The papers!" Mrs. Duke almost fainted again —and this time it would have been strictly involuntary.

"Now don't you worry," Josh pleaded. "I know lots of newspaper men and we'll have them keep this out. And you were right, Marjorie, and a swell kid for taking my part. Ivy's all right, but she had a drop too much. I told her not to mix her drinks."

"Oh, take me home, take me home," Mrs. Duke was saying.

Between them they got her out, and into the car. They nearly went off without Henry. When Josh saw him coming, running to get into the car, he was disgusted:

"Here comes that pest, Lawrence. Haven't you had enough trouble to-night without him?"

"Yes," answered Mazie-Beth icily, "but he happens to be my husband, so I suppose we'll have to take him. I'm glad we don't have any places like this in Hollywood. They wouldn't allow it."

But in spite of Josh's optimistic view practically all the papers had a line about it.

One of the yellow journals splurged:

**DUKE HEIRESS DEFENDS AGED ROUÉ IN GAMBLING BRAWL**

Beautiful Marjorie Duke, heir to fifteen millions, only daughter of Mr. and Mrs. Vincent Duke of this city, created a sensation at Bradley's, Palm Beach gambling resort, just before dawn Friday morning.

Screaming, "It was his—don't let them take his money!" the young girl hurled herself on the croupier in defense of Josh Huntington, retired oil magnate from Oklahoma.

In company with Mrs. Harry Brown (Ivy Brown —ex-chorus favorite) and an unknown man, the Duke heiress had gone to the famous gambling resort. Following a dispute with an unidentified person sitting next to him at the table, Huntington attempted to claim his winnings by force, and was set upon by the croupier.

Miss Duke defended her escort with cries of, "Don't give in, Josh. Don't let them make you a sucker."

On hearing the details of the brawl Mrs. Vincent Duke is said to have fainted in her palatial suite at the fashionable Breakers Hotel.

Lord Allan Fitz-Hamon, whose name has been linked with that of the beautiful Duke girl, and who is said to have sought her hand in marriage, was unable to be reached at his quarters at the Royal Poinciana early to-day.

* * *

Vincent Duke telephoned from New York. Unfortunately—or perhaps fortunately—the connection was bad:

"Is that you, Alice?"

"Vincent?"

"Is that you, Alice? What's that? I want Mrs. Vincent Duke. Is that you, Alice?"

"Don't shout, Vincent. I can hear you perfectly."

"Yes, but I can't hear you. What's that about a gambling den and Marjorie?"

"What?"

"I thought you could hear me."

"Say it again, and try not to mumble, Vincent. I don't hear you."

"I said gambling den. G as in George, A as in apple—"

"What was that you said about apple? I don't know any George in Palm Beach, what George? Prince George? Is he coming? What? Operator? You've cut off my husband. I can't hear anything. No, I won't excuse it. It was a New York call. . . . Marjorie, your father is just too impossible. I can't stand much more!"

Barely half an hour later a long straight message was put into Mrs. Duke's hands:

"I SAID GAMBLING DEN AND I MEANT GAMBLING DEN STOP I WANT TO KNOW WHAT YOU MEAN LETTING OUR DAUGHTER GO TO A GAMBLING DEN WITH JOSH HUNTINGTON AND AN UNKNOWN MAN AND A CHORUS GIRL STOP I SUPPOSE YOU WERE ENJOYING POOR HEALTH AS USUAL AND DID NOT KNOW IT STOP I DO NOT BLAME THE GIRL STOP I BLAME YOU STOP WIRE ME IMMEDIATELY STOP WHO IS THIS LORD FITZ HAMON QUESTION YOU KNOW MY OPINION OF IMPECUNIOUS PEERS STOP IF YOU CANNOT TAKE CARE OF MARJORIE AT PALM BEACH COME HOME STOP WIRE IMMEDIATE ANSWER

VINCENT"

And they weren't long in doubt about what Vincent Duke meant. The Eastern papers with their lurid stories were on the streets. Sensational journalism was handing itself a time.

Josh telephoned. Then Henry Lawrence. Then Allie. Mrs. Varney sympathized. There would have been more but Mrs. Duke had the telephone disconnected.

Somebody else was getting telegrams. Erskine Gander, in the same hotel, two floors below, was the recipient of many.

There was one from Chavreau, managing editor of the *Press:*

"SENT YOU TO PALM BEACH FOR NEWS NOT REST CURE STOP IF UNABLE TO WORK THERE ARE OTHERS STOP WHAT IS YOUR EXCUSE FOR BEING SCOOPED BY EVERYBODY ON DUKE HUNTINGTON BRAWL STOP MAKE IT GOOD YOU WILL NEED IT STOP ALSO WHY NOTHING ON DUKE FITZ HAMON ENGAGEMENT STOP ALL YOUR STORIES LOUSY LATELY STOP ARE YOU IN LOVE ANSWER

CHAVREAU"

Right after that came another, also from Chavreau:

"ARE YOU CRAZY STOP THIS IS A NEWSPAPER NOT A DETECTIVE AGENCY STOP ADVISE YOU GET NEWS ON FITZ HAMON AND QUIT ASKING US LOOK HIM UP STOP PUBLIC TIRED SHIRLEY SWAYNE FITZ HAMON STORIES GIVE US SOMETHING NEW STOP DUKE GIRL GOOD COPY VERIFY HER ENGAGEMENT

CHAVREAU"

Fitz-Hamon was Gander's first caller after the news broke.

"Thanks, old man, for keeping me out of it."

"Out of what?" Goose asked.

"Out of that gambling altercation the other night at Bradley's. It was deucedly decent of you to leave my name out. You know I can't afford that sort of thing."

Goose stared amazedly at Lord Allan Fitz-Hamon. "But I didn't have a thing to do with it. You don't mean to say you think I put that rot in about Marjorie and Huntington? Damn it, what do you take me for?"

"But everybody thinks you did. You're a newspaper man, aren't you?"

"You've a funny idea of a newspaper man."

"I've met several. Sorry if I hurt your feelings, old man," Allie sneered.

"Hurt my feelings! Get the hell out, will you? I'd write a thing like that about Marjorie Duke! Get out."

"I've no wish to remain. I came in a friendly spirit. I should have known better."

Bang, the door.

"Now I've muffed something else," Goose said to himself, as he stared at the door through which his distinguished visitor had just gone.

Obeying an uncontrollable impulse he telephoned Marjorie and getting no answer he went up to the suite. "This isn't the first gate I've crashed," he thought bitterly. "If I have to knock it in I'll get in and explain to that girl—"

He didn't even wait for the elevator, ran up two flights of stairs and arrived breathless and excited, at the entrance to Suite 1067.

Immaculately groomed, calm, poised as usual, stood Allan Fitz-Hamon at the door.

It was just opening. Annie was letting him in.

## CHAPTER V

THERE are times when it pays to risk getting thrown out in line of duty, and there are times when it doesn't. This, to Erskine Gander with seven hectic years of newspaper work behind him, seemed like one of the times when it doesn't.

So he let the Duke door close behind the distinctive back of Allie Fitz-Hamon, and retired to a back stairway to think.

On a comfortably carpeted step midway between the eighth and ninth floors he sat himself down to have a quiet cigarette. There's nothing like a hotel stairway for quiet. No telephone. No traffic. No noise of next door radio or gin party.

"Well," said Gander to himself, "here I am in a fine jam. I've been in others before, but this looks like the best yet. The paper is ready to fire me, and no wonder. They send me off with a roll of bills that would choke a horse, to settle down at the Breakers, and get all the inside news on the high and mighty. Settle? That's what I did, all right. Here I am eating my head off, and sending in the lousiest drivel that was ever filed in any telegraph office anywhere in the U. S. A.

"And all because I fell for a face. My God. Me. At my age. Twenty-eight, going on twenty-nine, and I'm still falling for faces.

"I got canned from the *Seattle News* for putting that waitress who got mixed up in the Sterling rape case on a train and telling her to keep her mouth shut. And did she? She did not! She got off at Spokane and dictated the story of her life to the guy from the *Express*.

"I got fired from the San Francisco *Tribune* on account of the red-headed jane from Marquard's. I was going to keep her fair name out of the dirty newspapers too.

"As late as last August I was thrown out on my ear from the Chicago *Trib* for permitting the girl from the *Sun* to sell me that line about being a cub. And after I let her in on the Du Paine shooting instead of keeping it exclusive, she turns out to be an old battle-axe thirty-five years old—with eighteen years in the game.

"That's what I know about women. Do I learn? Not me. I'd better quit before they fire me again. Perhaps I can get Dad to give me a job in the pulp mills. Maybe they've got some nice easy machine I can learn to run. I can change my name to Ole, and forget it's Gander.

"Oh, hell, what's the use. I'd just fall for some dame in the camp kitchen. I'd think she was misunderstood.

"What did I ever see in this Duke baby? A pair of innocent blue eyes, and a mouth that quivers. Right away I see her as a sensitive soul. Red Riding-Hood about to be set upon by the wolves of Palm Beach.

"Red Riding-Hood, my eye. If there's anything in heredity she's got the soul of a pig-sticker, and the mind of a stock- and bond-broker. Old Daddy Duke has coined more cash and robbed more widows and orphans in a nice refined, safe way than anybody else I can think of, offhand. And old Mammy Duke. Hypochondriac, trying to make up in pills for what she'd like to have in sex or limelight. Going in for Swedish masseuses for lack of anybody else to pinch her. Calling in all the Hindu boy Swamis in the state of Florida. Getting a second-hand kick selling her daughter off to the highest bidder. Trying to trade in the Duke millions for a coronet. God—it makes me sick. . . . That poor kid . . . there I go again. I might as well give up. Maybe I can get me a nice assignment covering Byrd's next expedition—no women to make a fool out of me at the South Pole.

"I'd better pull myself out of this and go see the Gibbons' social secretary about the damn masquerade ball. Helen's a good egg and she likes me. I'll scoop that. I'll have it down to the last caviar egg before any other hungry newspaper man gets his nose in the news. I may be a fool about women, but there are still a few that fall for the handsome Mr. Gander.

"I'd better go see what else the dick at the Cocoanut Grove has on Ivy Brown. She's been hanging around Allie Fitz-Hamon too. Dirty mess. Too bad I'm not in with a good old scandal sheet. What I know about that bimbo and his barnyard affairs would make good reading for those that like it. The way he left that little stock-actress from St. Paul to have that baby all alone in the County Hospital was just the lousiest deal I ever heard. Well, maybe he didn't know about it. Give the devil his due. She swore he didn't. Pluck! God, she was plucky. Good thing I wasn't around about then. I'd probably have offered to marry her to save her. Fitz-Hamon would have had a good laugh at my expense—damn his hide anyhow. Maybe he's mixed up with the liquor traffic here. A lot of damn swell looking Britishers are. They're in with the limey captains, don't you know, old top? Damn him. If he gets that sweet little Duke kid it's going to be Bluebeard all over again. He'll murder her spirit—kill her pride. If she knew what I know about his women . . . oh hell, it's none of my business.

"But I'd like to hang something on him. Damn his nerve coming to thank me for keeping him out of the papers. Him! I suppose he means it would break old Earl Whoosis' heart to have him mentioned in the same paragraph with roughneck Americans, wot? The Lady Thingamjig would pine away too. . . . Yeah. I'll bet he's phony. There I go again. I know he isn't phony.

"Well, get to work, Gander, old boy, get to work before you take root!"

With a last sigh, and a last puff of his stub of a cigarette, the reporter from the *New York Press* rose from his seat on the steps, and decided to walk on down to his room on the eighth floor.

At the landing of the eighth he had another idea. He'd go on up to the tenth and have another peek at the Duke's door. Maybe Allie had gone.

And halfway between the ninth and tenth when he was getting well out of breath, he stopped short.

Curled on the steps, having a good cry, was a girl in a blue silk sports dress.

He almost was on her before he could stop. It was Marjorie Duke!

She kept her head down, but he knew the top of her head.

Instantly he was beside her. "Marjorie! It's me—Goose! Oh, you poor little kid! It's a crime. Here, take my handkerchief—sure it's clean. Oh, I'm so sorry. Tell me what's happened—"

A muffled, "Nothing, thank you . . . please go."

"And leave you here alone? On the stairs? Marjorie, something *has* happened. You're hurt!"

"No—"

"Something's happened—"

"You know what's happened—" Still very muffled. A heartbroken sob.

That was too much for the susceptible Gander. With a capable pull of his long, muscular arm he gathered the limp blue silk figure into his lap.

And it was quite typical of the quixotic Goose that for the moment at least his interest was purely unselfish. Here was a damsel in distress. Here was he. Prepared to save her.

"Don't!" she cried angrily—beating two athletic

little fists on his chest—struggling back out of his lap, onto the stair.

"I should think you'd realize that you had made enough trouble, without—without this!" she panted.

There were tears in her eyes, tears that instantly overflowed, and went spilling down her cheeks.

Immediately Goose's eyes smarted, grew moist.

He took the handkerchief he had meant for her, and wiped his own eyes. After a moment Marjorie reached for it, and began to mop her tear-streaked, swollen face.

"You would be here," she said. "You've got a knack of being everywhere. It makes me sick." She began groping in the pockets of the sports dress, and retrieved a small gold compact after considerable trouble.

Goose remained silent while she powdered her nose, reddened her lips.

"For a friend, you treated me pretty shabbily," she said at last. "You did say you were my friend, didn't you?"

"Marjorie—of course. Listen—I—"

"That's what I thought. I hate to think what you'd have said in your dirty newspapers if you didn't like me!"

"Marjorie—"

"Don't Marjorie me. We might have been friends yesterday, but we certainly aren't to-day!"

"But—please! Oh, my God, how can I make you listen? Marjorie, I'm not responsible for everything that goes in every paper. I didn't write a word about that Bradley affair. I swear to God I didn't. I even talked Pyne and Harrison—two of the fellows—into keeping it out too, and they would have, if the yellow journals hadn't smeared it all over. Why, I almost got fired for *not* writing it—"

Her blue eyes studied his. "Truly?"

"True as you live. I've got the wire on me. From the managing editor, giving me hell." He began to dive through his pockets, bringing out dog-eared telegrams—none of which proved to be the right one—crumpled wads of copy paper, loose change, battered cigarette cases, stubby pencils, all the reporter's paraphernalia.

"Never mind. I believe you," she conceded grudgingly.

He went on searching. "I'll find it. I don't expect you to take my word for it. I was just up at your suite, to try to see you and explain and I saw Fitz-Hamon going in ahead, so I backed down the stairs. I had a smoke and was going back when I bumped into you."

She smiled, a watery little smile. "You must think I'm crazy—crying here on the steps. It was on account of Allie . . . oh, he didnt do anything! He came to see me, and I'd been crying—I've had so much trouble—Father's furious—and I wasn't going to see him, and Mother was determined I should and I knew she'd keep after me until I did, so I just slipped out, and I thought I'd wait till I was sure he'd gone."

"So you didn't want to see him!"

"Not then. I felt too awful."

"Oh. I see." Goose's momentary cheer departed, leaving him glummer than ever. "Well, go on. Let's have the rest of the story. Maybe I can help."

Marjorie shook her head, but she edged a little closer, put a friendly little hand on the young man's knee. "No—nobody can help. But it is nice to have someone to talk to. I—I get all bottled up. Did you ever get all bottled up—Mr. Gander?"

"Goose!"

"Well, Goose, then. Did you?"

He sighed. "Yes. I guess I have been sorta tied up in a knot. Go on, Marj—we'll hash this thing out. You think you're in love with Allie Fitz-Hamon, and you're afraid this little notoriety will spoil it. That's it, isn't it?"

She nodded. The tears gathered again.

"I thought so."

They fell silent again. Goose struggled with his own unhappy thoughts. Marjorie struggled with her tears. They got the best of her. She was soon sobbing again. Choking, racking, painful sobs.

"That's the real thing, all right. She's in love with the blighter," Goose thought, disconsolately. For a few miserable moments he sat there, feeling useless, watching her cry. Then he couldn't stand it any more. He took her into his arms again, and this time she didn't struggle. She just lay there, with her head on his shoulder, his big handkerchief squeezed to a damp ball in her hand.

"Poor little kiddie . . . poor little Marj. . . . Oh, don't cry, honey. . . . Gee, you'll have me crying too. Buck up."

"I—c-can't—"

"Sure you can—listen, this isn't—"

"Oh, you don't know—you don't know how I f-feel!"

"Yes, I do—I—I've been in love myself."

She sat bolt upright, wiping her wet eyes with the back of her wrist, "Oh, Goose, you're so wonderful! I'd just die if I didn't have you to talk to. I feel so much better. Goose . . . you won't ever give me away, will you? Mother . . . everybody . . . oh, you wouldn't, would you?"

He took her frightened face in his hands. "Honey, I won't ever give you away. Believe me?"

She looked off. "I believe you," she said slowly.

Another long silence.

"I've been thinking," he said at last. "Truly, things aren't so bad. The best thing to do is to ignore the whole thing. Everybody knows what the yellow journals are. Nobody with a grain of sense believes the stuff they print. Why, Marj, you could have had something just as damaging printed about you without any cause at all. Besides, anything—truth or lies—printed in a paper is here to-day and gone to-morrow. In ten days the same people who oh'd and ah'd over that story about you will have forgotten it."

She looked at him, her wide blue eyes half believing, half doubting.

"Just like a baby, smiling through her tears. Goddamit I'm the original sap!" Goose raged inwardly, and he snuggled her closer, and began to stroke her soft dark hair. . . . "Hell, I shouldn't touch her, I'm feeling worse every minute. Pretty soon I'll be best man at her swell wedding to Fitz-Hamon . . . no, I'm flattering myself, they'll bar the newspaper men—the Lady McGimple Mc-Thingumabob will see to that. Damn him and his ladies!"

"But Allie—" she whispered.

There it was. Allie. He cursed, as only a seasoned newspaper man can curse—in his mind. And aloud he said, "Don't worry about Allie. He's too much the man of the world to let a thing like that bother him."

"But his f-family—"

"Nuts! His family won't hear of it. Won't pay any attention if they do. Don't you worry, honey. If you want to be Lady Fitz-Hamon you'll be it—you just depend on what I'm telling you."

"Oh, Goose! Do you really think so?"

"Yeah." He couldn't say any more just then. The love in her eyes unmanned him.

Another long pause.

"But there's more than that. My father. He's funny. He just hates the English. And he thinks that anybody with a title is just after my money. You can't convince him. Isn't that funny?"

"Killing."

"But I'm serious!"

"I know, honey. So'm I."

"And, Goose . . . I know that Allie has had . . . you know, affairs—with women. With Shirley Swayne, and Lady Mawson and . . . and others. Father would hate that—"

"Wouldn't you?"

"No, of course not. Do you think I'm still a schoolgirl? I know that men like Allie Fitz-Hamon have had affairs. . . . Don't they all—?"

"I suppose so."

"Haven't you?"

"You flatter me."

"But you do understand. You didn't expect me to be shocked, did you?"

"No. I tell you, Marj. I've a kind of a head this morning. Don't feel too well. Got a lot of bad news, and so on. Suppose you go on back to your rooms. Allie will be gone by now."

She stood up. "Goose, I'll never be able to thank you. You're the nicest person I ever knew . . . except Allie! Here—" She stepped over and kissed him on the forehead, as he stood below her on the stairs. "That's to seal it. Why, you're blushing! Goose! Aren't you funny!"

"Funniest guy in the newspaper racket. Well,

good-bye, Marj, and you call me if I can help any time. Good luck with his lordship. Bye!"

Goose was on his way downstairs. The things he said to himself can not be repeated. But his parting thought, just as he entered his own door, might stand repetition. He said to himself: "And not only am I the goddamnedest fool in the world, but I've done the thing I'd have given my right eye to prevent. I've sold her on the Allie idea, if . . . she needed any selling.

"Well, never you mind, Allie, old top. I'll lay off your ladies, but just let me catch you in bootlegging and I'll spread your story pretty. She'll get over it. Girls don't die of love. If there's anything wrong with you I'll find it. If there isn't, maybe I'll plant something. Maybe I'll let you murder me—I wouldn't mind being the interesting corpse if I were sure you'd swing for it, you pretty-faced limey!"

Upstairs Mrs. Duke was waiting.

"I didn't know where you had gone. We waited and waited. You're just like your father, always disappearing, mysteriously. Never around when you're wanted. But it's just as well. Lord Allan practically declared himself. I hope you realize what a fortunate girl you are."

"Oh, Mother! No! Did he really! Oh—I'm so happy—you're sure? He really said—"

"Practically. There, that's enough, my dear. Don't lean all over me. You must remember that I'm not strong."

"But, Mother . . . but oh . . . what will Father say?"

"You may leave that in my hands."

"But you know how Father is—"

"That will do, Marjorie. When it comes to an issue, and I want something, I have it. And if you were more like me, my dear, you would know how to handle your father yourself. Your father is not one to hold out when he sees that your heart is really set on it."

"But, Mother—"

"That's all right, dear. Everything will be arranged. Just do your part and there will be nothing to worry about."

"But, Mother—"

"I feel so relieved—so relieved. I've worked so hard, and I'm not strong. Tell Annie my brown pills in the square box are almost gone, will you, Marjorie?"

Goose was calling at the Gibbons' home. He was calling on Helen Ilderton, the social secretary. A nice girl, and good-looking without her horn-rimmed glasses. Somebody must have told her she looked well in them. Goose had often considered telling her how much prettier she would be without them, but he had never quite gathered courage.

"What's all this about the ball? I understand the Follies can't be here in time—"

"Why, Goose! How did you find that out?"

"So it's true, eh? I thought so!"

Miss Ilderton, for once, was not amused. "I consider that taking an unfair advantage. You know I've favored you more than I should, already."

"Oh, Helen, don't be mean. Gosh, I've got a head on me, and everything's wrong. My paper is down on me. I've just got to get something on this. Come on—let's go to the Puritan and have a couple of drinks. Can you get away?"

"To the Puritan?" Miss Ilderton was really pretty when she laughed.

"Yes, haven't you ever been there?"

"Isn't it a rather naughty place?"

"All the way you look at it. Get your hat."

"Which hat? What does one wear to the Puritan?"

"Anything. What you've got on is fine. That's the advantage of it. It's the only place in Palm Beach where you can have any fun without dressing up!"

Trying to get his mind off Marjorie, Goose rather overdid the business of being nice to Helen Ilderton. They arrived at the pier, flushed and laughing —"As if we'd had the drinks already!" Helen said.

One of the sturdy little launches which take you out beyond Uncle Sam's twelve mile limit, to the four-masted Puritan—ex-lumber schooner—was ready to start. They scrambled aboard, with a motley crowd of a dozen others.

It was almost five—already too dark to recognize faces. Helen and Goose found seats in the stern and laughed and giggled all the twelve bobbing miles through the pale jade waters of the gulf stream.

"Looks like an arsenal. Are you sure it's safe?" Helen grinned, as they entered the cabin and a tall buccaneer, carrying a tray loaded with mugs of frothing beer, passed them by.

"Safe and better than two percent. Let's get a table and have some."

So they got the table and had first one, then two, then three mugs. After that Goose lost count.

Sitting there in the dim cabin, made over to represent a pirates' den, Helen talked on and on. She had brought the guest list for the Costume Ball and gave it to him to copy. She disclosed the sacred secret that it was going to be a Convicts' Ball.

"Mr. Gibbons is crazy about convicts since he's been going to all the crook plays in New York. We're going to have the guests wear stripes, and have them mugged, and everything."

"Quite appropriate."

"Goose, you're drunk!"

"No, my dear, only tight. I hear every word you're saying." Which was strictly true. Goose was too much the newspaper man to miss a story.

One half of his beery brain was fondly thinking about the rather attractive girl opposite him. He regretted her horn-rimmed glasses. He regretted that she was a little taller than he. He regretted that she was not Marjorie. With a distinct effort he could make himself think, for moments at a time, that she was Marjorie. At such times he achieved a look of lover-like adoration that really thrilled her.

But the other half of his brain was receptive, alert. He was remembering every word she said, and storing it away for future reference. This was a real scoop. . . . The Gibbons' guest list, for the annual Gibbons' ball, the social event of the season, was almost equivalent to a Palm Beach Who's Who. That Convict idea would make good copy too. . . .

"Want to dance?" he asked.

Helen shook her head. "No—too many drunks. They step all over you. Look at that awful fat man—he's going to fall!"

Goose followed her disgusted gaze. The fat man was not only going to fall, he did fall. It was Josh Huntington. Ivy Brown, dancing with him, narrowly averted going down with him.

"Who-oo! Josh! Get up and come sit with us! Bring Ivy!"

"Don't bring them to our table."

"Why, that's Josh Huntington. You've got him on your list. He's that big oil maggot—magnate, from Oklahoma. He looks lousy, but he's received by all the best people. That's Mrs. Harry Brown with him. Used to be in the Scandals. She did a Burmese dance, all dressed up in a big hat effect, and anklets . . . well, that was about all she wore . . . except gold paint. Shh . . . here they are. . . ."

"Young man, I see you everywhere I go. Are you shadowing me? Trying to get a line on my Past?" Josh winked at his blond companion, and poked Goose playfully in the ribs.

Helen sat stiffly, waiting for the introduction, which failed to come. Ivy sat down and addressed her as "Dearie." Josh offered to kiss her, and waved a fat hand pleasantly when she declined. "Brigand! More beer!" he shouted. "This," he added, "is the only place I know where you can call a waiter by his right name."

"By the way, Miss Ilderton is Gibbons' social secretary, did you know that?" Gander asked.

"Hell, no," said Josh. "Pleased to meet you, Miss Ilderton. Meet another nice girl, Ivy Brown. Ivy, shake hands with Miss Ilderton. You ought to know her." He leaned confidentially across the table to Helen. "Does he treat you well? I've never liked Gibbons myself. He only invites me to his balls because he has to. Maybe I won't go."

"Never mind, Josh. Drown your sorrows," Ivy advised, "and I'll have another myself. This is rum-runners' row and we came here to do some serious drinking."

"How are they running to-day?" Josh queried Goose. "Any bootleggers in the can?"

"Nobody of any importance just now . . . why? Do you know anything about the ring, Josh?"

But Ivy had her arms about his neck, and despite an appealing look from Helen, Goose had to dance with her.

"How do you like my girl friend?" Josh asked, as soon as the dancers were gone.

"I'm not used to people like her," Helen answered, stiffly. "Perhaps if I knew her better—"

"Aw, climb down off the high horse. She's all right. Don't get sold on this society stuff just because you're whosit's secretary. They think they're good because they can count back five generations. That's about as far as any American family likes to count. And give Ivy five generations and she'll be as snooty as any. Society's just a big mug—like my beer. Now you see the bubbles, now you don't. Now the Gibbons are bubbling. Pretty soon Ivy's children . . . oh hell . . . you get in deep with all these serious arguments. Tank up!"

So well tanked was Josh that by the time they were ready to leave they had difficulty in getting him down the gangway and into the waiting launch.

The tide was changing, making little eddies all

about them, and almost before they knew what had happened, another launch warped alongside, narrowly missing ramming them.

There was an exchange of profanity between skippers.

"Damn rum runners, never look where they're going," the Puritan's landing officer complained.

The searchlight on the Puritan's launch illuminated a long, narrow boat, piled high with cases. Only one face was shown distinctly.

Josh clutched Goose's arm, "That's the fellow that took my stake at Bradley's the other night!"

"No! Is it! A rum runner at Bradley's!"

"Doesn't look any more like that man than I do!" Ivy cried. "Josh, you're plastered."

"Plastered nothing. I distinctly saw him. I never forget a face."

"I wish you'd forget that one. I'm getting a little tired of that story. I wish you'd take me some place where you don't start a fight. I'm no publicity hound. I'll never live down that mess you got me into the other night."

"Come, Goose—get me home quickly," Miss Ilderton begged as soon as the little boat docked. "I've been away too long!"

"I'm afraid you didn't have a very good time,"

Goose said apologetically, as they were being wheeled along the ocean front. "But I'll make it up to you, Helen. We'll go somewhere nice, and dance. Let's see, how about—"

"How about what?"

Goose had forgotten to finish his sentence. He forgot to finish it now.

Under a palm tree, partly screened by a pile of boxes a familiar figure caught his eye, for one fleeting instant.

Allan Fitz-Hamon. The name flashed to his mind. Could it be Allie? There was something about the man's posture. The easy grace of the tall, athletic figure. . . .

It must be!

"Hey!" he called to the Negro who was rapidly pushing them by. "Stop a minute, will you?"

## CHAPTER VI

THE colored boy stopped pedaling.

"Whatever is the matter?" Helen asked.

"Nothing. Thought I saw someone I knew. Go on, boy!"

"Yas sah!" the boy—who must have been nearly sixty—drawled.

Goose was a little abashed. He realized that even if the tall man were Fitz-Hamon, even if he had something to do with liquor smuggling, this was not the time to approach him.

"I don't mind your using the information I gave you," Helen said, as they came up to the Gibbons' door, "but don't let it be traced to me."

"Darling, wild horses couldn't drag it from me!" was the newspaper man's stereotyped reply.

"You're a nice boy, Goose. I'll slip you an invitation. Want to come?"

"Want to come? You're great! And Helen—old Josh wants to bring his Ivy. Can you fix that? Mrs. Harry Brown, the Alba?"

Helen hesitated. What was a guest or two more?

"The old lady would kill me if she knew, but I'll do it for you, Goose. Just Mrs. Brown? Don't you want to let her old man in on it too?"

"Might as well. He'll add class. I hear he's a big shot. Well, I've got to get along. See you soon, Helen!"

She stood, a tall thin figure with eyeglasses, looking after him wistfully.

Goose sighed, as he was wheeled away. "It's always the wrong women that fall for a fellow. Hell, why couldn't it have been Marjorie?"

He was feeling pretty low by the time he reached the Breakers. He stood a long time, ringing the night bell. Gay place, Palm Beach, they roll in the sidewalks at midnight, he thought.

"Telegram for you, Mr. Gander," the night clerk said, handing him his key.

Goose flipped it open:

"YOUR SERVICES NO LONGER REQUIRED STOP TWO WEEKS SALARY IN THE MAIL. CHAVREAU, PRESS."

He read it over twice to be sure. He thought of Helen Ilderton and his scoop on the Gibbons' ball.

With muttered oaths Goose made his slow way to the elevator.

"Oh hell, what's the use?"

"You speakin' to me, sah?" the sleepy-eyed black boy inquired.

It was a hectic week for Marjorie.

Allie almost lived at the Breakers now. He was in attendance on her and her mother from noon until 'way after midnight every day.

They sunbathed at the Beach and Cycle. They lunched at the Country Club. Teaed at Cocoanut Grove and dined at Whitehall.

They were pushed in chairs, they visited friends aboard lantern-lit houseboats, they flew to Miami for the races in a friend's fast flying yacht. They skimmed the placid waters of Lake Worth in speed boats. They swam in the pool at Deauville, they golfed on the Everglades Links, and on the rare occasions when Allie had business elsewhere, Marjorie and her mother shopped in the fashionable Beaux Arts Arcade.

During all this time Mrs. Duke's health was perfect. She was tireless as a girl. She seemed to have forgotten all about the pills and the doctors and masseuses. Swarthy cheeked Swamis waited for her, patiently and futilely, in the lobby.

"You really don't need anything new, Marjorie, but Lord Allie is the sort of man to appreciate a woman's clothes. Not like your father who never knows whether you're wearing a sable coat or your grandfather's mackinaw."

Together they chose Chanel evening gowns, Jaeckel furs, Maria Guy hats, Schiaparelli sports things—all with a view to Allie's taste.

"It's too early to decide on a trousseau, but some of these things—"

"Oh, Mother! You embarrass me when you say things like that. He *hasn't* said anything to me—"

"Don't be absurd, my dear. It's in every paper."

"But it isn't true!"

"That's the way these things are made true. Marjorie, will you learn to trust me? Surely, with all my social experience—"

Many were the sleepless nights that Marjorie devoted to reflecting on her mother's social experience. Had she had any real social experience? True, she'd been all over the world—all the smart places at the smart times. St. Moritz in January, Cannes in February, Rome in April, Madrid in May, Deauville in July, Biarritz in September, home in time for the opening of the Metropolitan in November. And she'd been presented at Court.

But was that social experience? What did she know of the Newport that Josh Huntington talked about, of Allie's Mayfair, of the people who go to Aiken and Bar Harbor?

Would she know the way a man like Allie felt about these things? The way Allie's family would feel? Did Allie's attentions mean anything at all? Was he the right type of peer?

In all the time they had been together, not one word of love, nor a promise of such, had she had from him.

"Men don't make passionate love to the women they intend to marry," Mrs. Duke had said.

Yes, but did she know?

Night after night, Marjorie tossed on her pillow. Hot chocolate and whipped cream couldn't comfort her any more. Neither could caramels.

Why didn't Allie say something? How could he help it if he really liked her? She just ached to kiss him. Why, Erskine Gander had taken her into his arms and kissed her, and he wasn't the least bit in love with her. Why didn't Allie do something to show he cared—some little teeny, tiny thing?

She'd have liked to ask Goose; she felt sure he'd tell her the truth, but there wasn't any way of meeting him, privately. Whenever she saw him she was with Allie except once when she was lunching with Mazie-Beth in Phipps Plaza, and then he was with a girl. A big girl who just missed being pretty, and was quite a bit taller than he. They looked so silly when they danced together. You'd think he'd pick out a girl his own height, to pay so much attention to. . . .

It was on a Thursday, window-shopping alone on Via Parigy—which was like a corner of Barcelona with its odd passages, tiled alleys, balconies and strange winding stairways—that for the first time she met Goose alone.

He was just coming out of a telegraph office, looking particularly bright and cheerful.

"Oh, Goose! I'm so glad to see you. I've been wanting to talk to you for a week. Are you busy? Can we have lunch or something?"

"Sure, let's go into the Purple Bougainvillea, it's right round the corner. This is fine, meeting you! It gives me a chance to celebrate my new job!"

"New job?"

"Yeah, I got fired from the old one. Lost my head over a beautiful girl."

"Oh, Goose! Why did you?"

"Oh, I fell for a blue-eyed baby. She didn't even like me. So now I'm working for a yellow journal. You better look out, Marjorie!"

"Goose—you don't mean it."

"Oh, yes I do. I'm working for a tab, and I'm out after all the news that the *Press* didn't think fit to print. But don't you worry, Marjorie. I never learn. I'll still look out for my friends. What'll you have, terrapin or barracuda?"

"Neither! I've been living on both for a week."

"How about chile con and banana shortcake? Go as far as you like on four-fifty. I think I have four-fifty. Yes. I have, and enough for a tip."

"Oh, Goose, you're so different from everybody else. I hardly know you at all, and I feel as though I had known you all my life. Can I tell you my troubles?"

"Your father won't consent?" Goose ventured hopefully.

"No, it isn't that. I know that Father won't stand in the way of my happiness. He might make a fuss but he'd give in. It's Allie. . . . I'm afraid he doesn't love me."

Goose reached hastily for a glass of water. "This darn chile is hot. You don't mean that about Allie. He's crazy about you, Marj. Gosh, he's been with you every day this week."

"Yes, but—oh, Goose, this sounds so silly—but he's never even kissed me."

"Hasn't he? Fine!"

"Oh, don't tease me. I'm serious. I love him so."

Goose finished his chile. "I don't know, Marj," he said at last. "I don't know what to tell you to do. But there's one thing—Allie is a lot more likely to be in love with you and not kiss you, than to kiss you and talk about love later. I wouldn't worry, Marj—I guess it's all set, all right. You'll get married, and move upstage, and then I never will see you."

"But we'll always be friends, Goose—always and always."

"You promise to be a sister to me?"

"Don't joke, I mean it. I will always be your friend, Goose, and I hope I'll always see you—often."

He squeezed her hand. "You dear kid. Listen. I've got an hour before I have to go to work. Come for a ride with me?"

"I'd love to, but suppose we run into Mother—you know she—"

"Yes, I know all about Mother. But we'll go the other way."

They followed Worth Avenue down to the Atlantic. Goose had the boy pedal them into Gus's Baths.

"Here's one place I've never been."

"Lots of places you've never been," her escort smiled.

At this hour in the afternoon the place was almost deserted. They lay under a striped umbrella and gazed out at the line of surf breaking on the beach.

"Palm Beach is darn romantic at that, Marj."

"In the moonlight?"

"No, it's really a great place, only nobody ever takes time to look at it. Flagler knew his onions."

When Marjorie looked up at him he went on, "I wish I'd been one of the Florida East Coast stockholders. Way back in the gay nineties old Henry M. bought everything he could lay his hands on around here. He knew it was good agricultural land, but he had his own ideas about advertising. He sold the idea of wintering down here under the palms, to all his rheumatic cronies. He thought they'd put up a few winter shacks and go into agriculture. But look what happened. All they raise around here now is peanuts and hangovers. I wish I had a drink right now. Josh puts gin in cocoanut milk. . . . By the way, did you ever hear the cocoanut story?"

"Is it about the Four Marx Brothers?"

"Better than that. It's about an old sailor with

a shipload full of cocoanuts. They got lost in a storm, and the ship broke up. All the little cocoanuts drifted ashore and grew in rows all along the beach."

"You're fooling!"

"No—solemn truth, and this concludes my bedtime story for to-night. I've got to get back to work."

"Oh, let's not go yet. I want to talk to you some more."

"Allie will talk to you, honey. Come along. I'm a working man. I'll have to send you home alone—I've got a man to see. Be a good girl!"

"But, Goose—there's so much more I want to talk to you about—please—"

"Next time. You don't want me to get fired again, do you? I like to keep a job a week or two. Bye, Marj. Take her to the Breakers, boy!"

He waved after her, watching the slim figure in white grow smaller and smaller, until it was lost in a swarm of chairs coming and going along the road.

"She's adopted me, all right," he thought bitterly. "I'm just like an aunt to her. Well, it's all right. I wouldn't marry a girl like that anyway. It isn't pure cussedness that sets me on Fitz-Hamon.

If he's all right he shouldn't mind my sniffing around, and if he isn't I'll show him up. Then if Papa Duke wants little Marjorie to marry a high class bootlegger—*all right!*"

So Marjorie Duke went back to the Breakers, and Erskine Gander, newspaperman, slipped by inconspicuous back alleys known only to himself and his kind, into certain Palm Beach places not mentioned in Chamber of Commerce blurbs. He considered it a rare stroke of luck that his brand new employers had assigned him to work on Rum Runners' Row.

Which was one of the reasons why Helen Ilderton, the Gibbons' social secretary, wasn't able to reach him at his usual haunts.

Helen had suffered qualms of conscience. She had regretted mailing the invitation to Mr. and Mrs. Harry Brown at the Alba.

What a silly she was!

"Are you sure Mr. Gander is not there? You've had him paged? . . . Yes, if he comes in, have him call Miss Ilderton. . . ."

Helen had no plans, but she depended on Goose. Newspapermen had nerve enough for anything. He got her into this mess, now he'd have to get her out of it, even if he had to get into the Brown woman's room, and swipe the invitation.

"He'll do something. He'll find some way out," she thought, trying not to worry. But the afternoon slipped by and no word from him.

She telephoned the Alba.

Mrs. Harry Brown was not in her room.

Helen heaved a sigh of something like relief. Maybe she hadn't received the invitation yet. Maybe Goose could get it before she saw it.

Poor Helen. She, too, was in love. She, too, had her troubles.

Josh was bringing Ivy home from the Poinciana Grill.

"Tell him to drive me straight to the Alba, Josh. I'm awfully tired."

"The Alba! Now look here, baby, you distinctly said that you'd come back to the Whitehall with me."

"Not to-night, Josh, dear. I'm tired. Terribly tired."

"You're being tired a lot lately. I'm getting tired too. I'm a good-natured slob, but I'm not a sucker. The Whitehall, boy."

"The Alba, boy!"

The chair came to a full stop under a lamp. The boy scratched his head. "Yesh, sah, yesh, ma'am."

"The Whitehall!"

"No, Josh—please. The Alba, boy! Josh, I've got to get home. I'm expecting a telephone call from my husband. . . ."

"Sure you don't mean Allie Fitz-Hamon?"

"Josh, I've told you that my interest in Allie is purely platonic."

"You've had a lot of platonic business with him lately then. You've got to cut it out. I'm not going to buy diamond bracelets for Allie Fitz-Hamon's women. Besides, you might have the finesse to stay out of that. The little Duke girl is going to announce her engagement."

"Really? That's interesting. I've never thought of Allie as the marrying kind."

"Oh, he'll marry fifteen million without a shotgun."

"I suppose so. The girl wouldn't have a chance without her money. She's pretty, yes. But what's that? Hundreds of them in every five and ten. Flo Ziegfeld wouldn't give her a second look!"

She was a little ashamed of her vehemence, after Josh, a little glum, a little thoughtful, had obediently left her at the door.

She shouldn't have talked like that to Josh. He had a right to be annoyed with her. And why did she have to get catty about the Duke girl? She shouldn't object to Allie's taking a wife. . . . She had a husband. . . .

Ivy laughed out loud when she thought of that. She had an infectious, genuine laugh. It amused her to remember her married state. Nobody would believe it, but she had been married for fifteen years, and loved her husband!

She poured herself a generous two fingers of Scotch in her toothbrush glass and turned to her mail. Ivy's mail was never very interesting. She herself never wrote letters, and her admirers thought it safer to see her rather than to write to her. She glanced over the usual ads, hotel and night club announcements, and bills. There was a large, creamy white envelope at the bottom of the pile. The invitation to the Gibbons' Fancy Dress Ball.

"Hmmmm," said Ivy. "Hmmmmm."

She got up and poured herself another drink of Scotch. Four fingers, this time.

She examined the envelope. "Mr. and Mrs. Harry Brown." Was someone horsing her? Was it Josh's idea of a joke? For some moments she sat, plump hands with long pointed pink nails, toying with the envelope. Then she went to the telephone and called a North Palm Beach number.

"Is Louie there? . . . Call him. I want to talk to Louie. . . . Tell him it's Ivy. . . . Hello, Mr. Harry Brown! How's the kid? Feeling younger every day? Fine. Listen, you're invited to the Gibbons' Ball. With your wife, Mrs. Brown. What? . . . Yes, I knew you were going, honey boy. I'm just telling you you're invited. Waiter nothing. I tell you you're going to be a guest. . . . No, I don't know how. Josh, I guess. He's a great little old fixer. Well, you can rent a pair of coat-tails, can't you?

"Listen, when can I see you? No—nothing serious. Allie is acting up. Pig-headed. Won't listen to reason. Yellow? Not that one, Papa. He's just so close to fifteen million that he can't think in small change. . . . No, I don't want to come there. You better meet me some place. How about the Breakers Casino? It's public enough there. Make it ten o'clock. Toodle-oo, darling!"

## CHAPTER VII

THE papers were full of the Gibbons' Jail Frolic. Erskine Gander's tabloid broke the news, and the rest followed anywhere from thirty-two minutes to thirteen hours later.

Disappointed climbers read the guest list, and cursed their luck and the Gibbons' social secretary.

Successful contenders ordered copies mailed to friends. One deliriously happy matron had 150 marked copies in the mail before sundown. She was under the sad impression that Palm Beach success would help her crash the sacred portals at Newport.

Ivy Brown, having a late breakfast in bed, in her jade and gilt suite at the Alba, let her coffee cool while she read the list. Her name was not mentioned. She laughed and kissed a pretty hand in the direction of her dressing table, on which, amid the confusion of scent bottles, gold-backed brushes, and spilled powder, lay a square creamy envelope addressed to Mr. and Mrs. Harry Brown.

Mrs. Gibbons, herself, telephoned the costume people who had been commissioned to supply the prison outfits. She screamed, she scolded, she ranted. They had, she told them, ruined everything, by letting the story get to the press.

Helen Ilderton, a little paler, a little more pinched-looking than usual, took her share of the storm calmly. "You can't keep anything as colossal as one of your balls out of the papers, Mrs. Gibbons. Too many people know about it. Caterers, costumers, stationers. I don't know how the leak happened, and I don't think we ever will. But I gave the guest list out myself. Wasn't that your wish?"

"No! You know how I dislike publicity, Miss Ilderton!"

"Yes, Mrs. Gibbons. But you know what happened last year when we withheld it. They printed such impossible lists, and we had such trouble."

Mrs. Gibbons remembered. Remembered all too well.

"Kindly respect my wishes in the future, Miss Ilderton."

"Yes, Mrs. Gibbons. I'm sorry."

When Erskine Gander finally got her message, and had time to see her, it was Friday noon.

Helen snubbed the impulse to cry on his shoulder. She was two or three years older and somewhat taller.

It wouldn't do.

He listened gravely while she told him, as calmly and quickly as she could.

"And so Mrs. Gibbons is furious with me. If she sees Ivy Brown she'll know she isn't on the list—"

"In a mob like that?"

"Oh, Goose! The notorious Mrs. Brown. That golden beauty of hers. . . . She's the first person you see, anywhere. . . . Oh, Goose . . . can't you help me?"

She bit her lip to stop its trembling.

"I feel like a louse," Goose groaned.

He watched her take off her glasses, to wipe them on a filmy handkerchief. Noticed how darn good-looking she was without them.

"Helen, old girl, there isn't a chance of pinching the bid from Ivy now, and I couldn't talk her out of going if I crawled on my knees. You don't know those ex-chorus girls. But I tell you what. I'll go see Josh. I'll get him to bring her late, and drag her out early. He's a good scout, he'll do it . . . and, Helen—"

Helen gulped. "Yes, Goose."

"I'll—I'll get you out of it somehow. I'll get you a better job—"

"There are no better jobs. It's the best one—"

"Well, I'll—I'll—you trust me, Helen. I'll fix things."

She looked almost beautiful as she smiled into his eyes. "I'll trust you, Goose. I know you won't fail me."

Goose groaned inwardly. "Now I'm in for it again. I'll be proposing to her in a minute. Oh why, oh why, didn't I keep out of this. . . ."

And aloud he heard himself saying, "Wait—I've got an idea."

Just what the idea was to be he didn't know. And then it dawned on him, bright and beautiful and fully formed as Aphrodite rising from the sea!

"This is good! Oh, this is a pip. Listen. You've got plenty of time to fix it. Go in for a bunch of little booths along the edges of the ballroom. Have the photograph gallery in one, and put a fortune-teller—you know, palm reader—in another, and here's the best yet—have somebody taking finger-prints in another one. . . . Have them go right through the prison routine. There's new stuff the papers haven't had. You wanted a surprise. There's a surprise for your old lady Gibbons. Prison barbershop and everything. Like it?—God, I ought to be a social secretary . . . sell that idea to your old lady. . . .

"Oh, there's no end to what you can do with that. You ought to get the Gibbons to hire me. Go on—run along—make yourself square."

Helen was already on her feet. Her cheeks were flushed. "I believe you've hit it. Oh, Goose! You darling! Mr. Gibbons will love the finger-prints. He wanted to have dungeons, only Mrs. Gibbons wouldn't let him. And your Mr. Josh can keep Mrs. Brown in the corners. . . . Oh, Goose—you *are* dear!"

Goose wiped a perspiring brow as he went back to his waiting chair. "Whew! I got out of that pretty well. Helen saves her skin, I save mine."

He gave the chair boy a dollar tip. It was a good world. He had had a congratulatory wire from his tabloid. He had a fine story on an Allan Boulder, Britisher, who might or might not be Allan Fitz-Hamon under an alias.

"The only thing that makes me doubt it," he said to himself, as he went in search of Josh Huntington, "is that I don't think the blighter has the brains to be a bootlegger."

Marjorie whistled to herself as she leisurely dressed for the Gibbons' Ball. She lay in her warm, jasmine-scented bath, and thought about Allie.

She thought she had never enjoyed anything so much as just lying there, sensuously sniffing the sweetness of the jasmine, relaxing in the warm, soft water, watching a big pale-green sponge float lazily toward her.

There's such a difference between just loving, and being loved. Marjorie felt beloved to-night. She knew that Allie loved her.

On the almost deserted sands at the Beach and Cycle Club he had suddenly leaned forward and kissed her, swiftly and gently, on her surprised, half-open mouth.

"Marjorie," he said, "I love you. You know that, don't you?"

It had all happened so fast she hadn't known just what to do or say. She hoped she hadn't seemed too eager, for he had laughed, and patted her hand and said, "There, I couldn't help that. But I'll not say any more until I've had the opportunity to talk to your parents." And then they both had caught sight of Evelyn Throckmarten and the Browning boy, coming over their way, and Allie had leaped to his feet and pulled her up and shouted, "Race you to the surf!"

And they had dived into the waves, and swum out beyond the Pier, Allie's bronzed shoulder and sleek fair head cleaving the water just ahead.

It was a long swim for a racing stroke. "Wait!" she had called, at last. "Wait for me!"

And Allie had turned over on his back and laughed, his white teeth flashing in the sun, and they had rested, floating and treading water, and then swum slowly, easily back to the beach.

"Marjorie!" Mrs. Duke called through the door. "Don't dawdle! Have you forgotten we have a dinner engagement?"

"No, Mother!"

Reluctantly Marjorie got out of her scented tub, began to dress.

Dinner engagement! Always something. That was the worst of Palm Beach. You never had time to really enjoy anything. You were always hurrying from here, to get there. You never could get away from people with someone you loved, because everywhere you went you met all the other people you knew.

Marjorie sighed. She'd have liked this perfect

hour all to herself, to think about Allie, but it couldn't be helped.

Ernestine had laid out her things on the bed. She slipped the supple ivory satin over her head, and stood motionless before the long glass, while Ernestine fastened it, arranged the soft, dully gleaming folds. It was the simplest gown she had. Her mother had chosen it to compliment her slim, delicately rounded figure, and to accentuate the loveliness of her jewels.

For the first time she was to be allowed to wear the diamond and emerald necklace and bracelets that had belonged to her grandmother, that Carlotta Duke who for a brief season dominated New York Society, dazzled and startled, took by surprise what had seemed an impenetrable fortress—before falling back again into the arms of the other rich, but unsuccessful, aspirants to social prestige.

It was a pretty girl who looked back at Marjorie from the long, hotel mirror. A girl who was slim, and young and starry-eyed.

She turned to reach for the box that held Allie's flowers. She knew the card by heart, but she read it again—"With fondest love, for the loveliest girl in the world, from her admirer, Allie."

"Such a disappointment," her mother moaned,

trailing into the room in fluttering chiffon and a fat rope of pearls. "Dear Allie won't be able to escort us to the Gibbons' to-night. He will be unavoidably detained."

"Oh, Mother!" Marjorie could have cried. Everything was spoilt.

"My dear, don't be so tragic. You'll see your beau soon enough!" Mrs. Duke was heavily playful. But to Marjorie, young, and in love for the first time in her life, the disappointment was almost unbearable.

They stopped for the Lawrences on the way.

"Why a prison party?" Henry wanted to know. "There's no point in it. Why all the fuss about the Gibbons and their ball?"

"Haven't you been reading the papers?" Mrs. Duke asked.

"I never read them. But why all the fuss about it?"

"Because it is the most exclusive party of the season—in a large way. . . . Look! There's the Baroness de Pierre and the Duke of Netherlands in the Hispano Suiza. They're going!"

The guests were arriving in cars, in bantams, in

chairs, even a red bug or two. Women in pale evening gowns. Men in dark coat-tails.

The Harry Stones—the William Goedbys—the Perry Leonards—the Brewster Sorchans—the Grandduchess Elisandre. The Guy Wagners—Madame de La Rochefoucard—the Earl of Eustace—the Stacey Kincaids—Colonel and Mrs. Tom White.

Their car was in a long line of Rolls, Vauxhalls, Peugeots, Bugattis, Mercedes-Benz. Reporters and cameramen swarmed the porte-cochère of the Gibbons' mansion.

"It looks like a preview at Grauman's Chinese Theatre," Mazie-Beth decided graciously. "Oh look, there's Shirley Swayne. Did you see her in the Storm? She was wonderful!"

At last they gained the door. Amid the boom of cameramen's flashlights they made their way into the hall. Tall footmen in the Gibbons' dark blue livery were lined along the wall.

Their knobby legs in white silk stockings caught Henry's eye. "Glad I don't have to wear plus fours!"

After they had disposed of their wraps, Charlie Gibbons' own valet handed them each the well-known striped prison costume. As they donned them in the dressing rooms, the numbers on the coats and skull caps were recorded by maids or footmen.

Josh Huntington, a red-faced elderly cherub in prison stripes, buttonholed Henry Lawrence. "Look. Can you beat my luck? I'm number 13."

"That's nothing, I'm 23!

"Come on, Huntington, let's get inside. They're taking photographs and thumb-prints in there. . . . What a bally silly thing! We had better ideas than that when I was a sophomore at Princeton. The costumes aren't even authentic. They're not using stripes any more. Don't you know that?" he added earnestly.

"Oh, come on, don't be high hat. The liquor's simply criminal—"

Marjorie and her mother, with Mazie-Beth Lawrence, had already made their way into the ballroom.

"Disgusting," Henry repeated, as he got his first glimpse of Palm Beach in stripes.

They were standing in line, as Richards announced each one in turn.

"It is rather a shame to spoil perfectly good Louis the Fourteenth bouisserie with canvas stone coverings," Josh agreed.

"Deucedly funny chap, this Gibbons. Where did you say the bar was, Josh?"

"Up this way," Josh tried to break through the line but Richards' firm arm intervened. "You must wait your turn, sir."

"Hell, I'll die of thirst! Why the prison discipline?"

But they had to wait and be announced, "mugged" and "thumbed" like the others, and after an interminable wait they reached the bar and got their drinks in prison tin cups.

"Half water!" Josh complained.

"The whole thing's a frost. I didn't want to come anyway."

"Well, let's try a Seventy-five before we give up," Josh advised.

This was better. Gin and champagne do raise the spirits. "The whole thing's a frost," Henry said, but with less venom. "Shall we look for the girls?"

A colored orchestra was warming up in the ballroom. "The chain gang," Josh grinned, "from the Dixie highway."

They found Mazie-Beth and Mrs. Duke waiting impatiently. But Marjorie had disappeared. She was dancing somewhere, Mrs. Duke said.

She was in reality sitting on a prison bench in what was yesterday the drawing-room, holding tight to Goose's arm.

"It's all right! He kissed me!" she was telling him childishly. "He really did—to-day, at the beach."

Goose did not look impressed.

"Oh, how stupid of me. Allie! Allie kissed me. Of course you didn't know what I was talking about!"

"Oh. Allie. That's nice. How did he do it? Show me!"

"Oh, Goose! You always tease me when I'm serious. I am serious, and there's something else I want to ask you. We're practically engaged, but he wants to talk to Father first, and when reporters ask me if we are, why I just don't know what to say. Of course I have to say there's no truth in it, but do you think it could hurt Allie's feelings? He's awfully sensitive. And, Goose, when they ask Allie things like that what do you suppose he says? He would have to deny it too, wouldn't he?"

"I suppose so," Goose said unhappily. He was feeling very low. His detective work along Rum Runners' Row had borne fruit, but not the right kind. He had uncovered two good stories, and put them on the wire for his tabloid, but he had also discovered that Allan Boulder was a portly Welshman, who did not in the least resemble Allan Fitz-Hamon. Allan Fitz-Hamon was, as he had suspected and hoped, known to Rum Row, but alas for Goose—purely as a customer, as you might be.

Until he had the proof of Allie's innocence he hadn't realized how desperately he was hoping for his guilt. Now there was nothing to prevent his marriage to Marjorie. He couldn't do anything to stop it. She'd be Lady Fitz-Hamon before the year was over, and the only girl he had ever loved . . . really loved . . . would be lost forever.

"I hope you'll be awfully happy," he said. "Fitz-Hamon's pretty lucky. You know, Marj—I could fall for you myself."

"Oh no, Goose. We're—we're different."

"Yeah. Just a couple of old family friends. Well, it's all right—I hope you're happy. I hope like the devil you're happy. I'll break Fitz-Hamon's neck for him if you aren't."

"Goose!"

"Well, I can't help it. I love you, Marjorie. Go on and laugh. It's funny. Ha, ha!"

"I'm not laughing," she giggled. "I mean I'm not laughing at you. I don't believe a word of it. You'd laugh at me if I did. But—quick—look at Josh Huntington. *What* is he doing?"

Goose groaned. Just his luck. Try to make a serious speech and somebody stages a comedy right away. Josh with a tape measure and notebook was pursuing Helen Ilderton, trying to measure her ankle.

"Bertillon measurements," he was shouting. "We've got to have them to make it complete."

Helen ran out the other door, the roaring Josh in hot pursuit.

Marjorie laughed out loud. "That's your girl, isn't it? Why don't you go and stop Josh? Aren't you jealous?"

"Marjorie! I've been looking all over for you! Come—we're all waiting for you!"

It was Allie, and without a word of greeting for Goose he had swept Marjorie to her feet and was away. But in that fleeting instant—one good look at Allie, a different Allie, Allie in convict's stripes—Goose had a disconcerting thought. A crazy thought. He knew it was crazy, but he couldn't help it—he had seen that face somewhere before attired just like that.

"My God," he thought, "it can't be. Allie Fitz-Hamon in the Rogues' Gallery! My memory's going haywire. No, I can't be wrong. I've seen him or his twin brother in that get-up. Where? Oh, where could it be? Oh, Goose, you're crazy . . . you had him a rum runner last week, and look what it got you. But this is different. I can't be wrong. I've known ever since I set eyes on the man that I'd seen him somewhere—and now I know what he was wearing when I saw him. I don't care if he is Lord Allie Fitz-Hamon and all that rot. That boy has been in the pen somewhere and I've seen him!

"Now how the dickens am I going to find out—"

"Oh, Goose! Are you saving this dance for me!" Goose jumped. He stared at Helen Ilderton stupidly.

"Don't you know me in my prison clothes? Doesn't everyone look funny! Did you see Mr. Varney! He's lost all his dignity. I'm really afraid to trust him with the silver, he looks so dangerous! Don't you want to dance?"

"Thanks, Helen. I'm working on a story."

"Oh, Goose! Nothing that will get me in trouble again, after I just got out!"

He grinned rather sheepishly. "I hope not. By the way, did the Harry Browns show up? What's Harry look like?"

"He didn't come. But she did, and I was terrified, but I needn't have worried, because Mrs. Gibbons has been playing long term contract bridge and the Boss— Oh, look—there they are—"

Pushing the rubber bars aside for his lovely companion, the portly Charles Hamilton Gibbons was leading the way into the more or less secluded drawing-room. He was obviously looking for a place to sit down.

Helen clutched Goose's arm. "Don't you love it? She hadn't been here seven minutes before he found her, and he's been with her every minute since. What will Josh Huntington say? But by this time I suppose he's asleep in a corner. He was chasing me around trying to take my measurements a while ago, and he could hardly stand then. The Seventy-fives were too much for him."

"Too bad," Goose said. He couldn't keep his mind on what Helen was saying.

The orchestra struck up the Prisoner's Song. Its wailing cadences floated to them from the ballroom.

"Look here, Helen, what are they going to do with all the mugs and thumb-prints now they have them?"

Helen glanced at the watch on her wrist.

"Thanks for reminding me. It's time to get them now. We're going to have the guests lockstep into the banquet hall, and they'll find their places by means of the photographs and finger-prints. We're using them for place cards. It was my idea—don't you think it's clever?"

Goose's brow was corrugated. He was concentrating on something.

"Didn't you hear what I said?" she laughed.

"I heard you. I was just going to ask if I couldn't get them for you, Helen. I haven't anything to do for twenty minutes."

Helen melted. "Oh no, thanks. They're just on top of my desk in the office. I have to go over that way to get to the Banquet Hall anyway. Thanks just the same—but never mind—"

"Oh, let me."

"No, don't bother Goose. . . . Now what's the matter with the lights? They're all flickering. If anything goes wrong Mrs. Gibbons will pin it on me. . . . Look—they're out!"

"No, they're coming on again."

They did—for a brief second. Then, with a half-hearted flare they died out completely. The place was in darkness.

"Let's get over to the ballroom," Goose said.

"Take my hand, I get all turned around in the dark." But she groped in vain for Goose—bumped her head on a door.

In the ballroom there were shouts and giggles, and high, half hysterical squeals. The music stopped. There was the sound of slow shuffling feet. A terrific jolt. "Look out where you're going!" a man's voice cried. A woman screamed.

In the card room Mrs. Duke laid down her hand. "How unique. You've thought of everything, Mrs. Gibbons."

Mrs. Gibbons got to her feet, groped her way toward the mantel where there were candles.

"I only wish I had," she said. "It's the extra lights. My secretary should have done something about it. I wonder if the servants have the extra fuses. Won't someone call Richards? He's so clever about electricity."

The clever Richards was already in the basement. In a few moments the lights flashed on again, almost blinding in their brilliance.

Henry Lawrence and Allie were helping Marjorie Duke to her feet. "It's nothing," she was laughing. "I'm not the least bit hurt."

"Clumsy bounder. He almost knocked Mazie-

Beth down too!" Allie glared around the room for the offender, but nobody seemed to be moving.

"Really, I thought he was going to tackle us," Henry Lawrence who was dancing with Marjorie, said. "I couldn't hold her—he knocked her right out of my arms!"

"You were hurt!" Mazie-Beth cried. "Marjorie, look at your wrist, it's bleeding!"

"I didn't know. I suppose I'm too excited to feel anything!"

Her eyes met Allie's, and she thought, "I don't care a bit—it was worth it to have him look at me like that." Her lip trembled. "I'm not hurt—really I'm not, Allie!"

"My poor child, we must find your mother. But wait—what's this?" He stooped and picked up her diamond and emerald bracelet, which had broken and fallen to the floor.

Marjorie gave an involuntary little cry. "Oh, I wouldn't have lost that for anything. They were Grandmother Duke's—"

Her hand groped to her throat . . . the necklace. . . .

Mazie-Beth's scream rang out, "It's gone! It's gone. Your diamond necklace!"

## CHAPTER VIII

THE crowd pushed closer with little cries of "What's happened?"—"Whose necklace?"—"Who's hurt!"

Allie had a protecting arm around Marjorie. "Stand back," he commanded. "Give her air!"

Josh Huntington went to fetch Mrs. Duke, who made him repeat the news twice before it penetrated. Then she fainted.

A detective blew a police whistle. Servants barred doors and windows. Charlie Gibbons mounted a chair, resting a fat hand, partly for moral support, partly in the interest of balance, on a detective's shoulder:

"My dear friends," he said, "we ask you not to leave the house until you have spoken to either Detective Eggers or myself. There has been a robbery. Miss Duke has lost a diamond necklace. We fear that there have been other losses. For your own protection and interest, as well as mine, I ask that you coöperate by filing in to see Detective Eggers and myself in the library. In the library! Thank you!"

"We'll have to get Mrs. Duke home!" Henry Lawrence was tugging at his host's coat. "And my wife. She's very nervous. And Marjorie Duke—"

"Mrs. Throckmarten can't wait either!" Throckmarten Senior raised his voice.

"No, no—nobody can leave!"

"Damned outrage!" Henry Lawrence protested. "This is always what happens when people go to insane lengths to provide excitement. We ape the criminal classes. A robbery follows. Exactly!"

"Henry, I want to go home," Mazie-Beth wailed, "and I've lost an earring. It was a genuine Tecla pearl!"

Out on Royal Palm Way, already three blocks off, Erskine Gander slowed down for breath. As he did so another panting figure puffed into sight.

"Where are all the chairs?" he wheezed.

"Can't you find one, either?" Goose panted. His quick mind jumped to a typical newspaperman's conclusion. Here was McLane of the *Post*, hoofing it as fast as he was. Something was up. He fell in step.

"There's no shorter way to Phipps Plaza, is there, Goose?"

"Phipps Plaza?"

"Yes—isn't that the nearest place to file a wire?"

"I suppose so. That's where I was heading for," Goose lied.

They slowed up at the County Way, and entered the Plaza barely puffing.

They arrived just as Western Union was closing. "Hey, there!" Goose shouted. "We've got to file fast wires for the press!"

He wondered what the wires would be about, and hung back, hoping McLane would say something.

He hadn't long to wait.

"What are you going to appraise the Duke girl's necklace at?" his colleague asked.

"Um. . . . I don't know. What do you think?" Marjorie's necklace. . . . Then the lights didn't go out accidentally . . . there had been a robbery, and Marjorie . . . good heavens . . . Marjorie. . . . "Say—she's all right? She wasn't hurt?"

"Sure, she was all right. Didn't you see her walking around afterward? But the old buzzard that lost the Cabochon ruby broke her leg when she fell downstairs."

"I didn't get that . . . I got out too quick. What's her full name?"

"I don't know. Mrs. Anthony D. I think—"

"D— what?"

"Anthony Drexel? Does that sound right? Mrs. Anthony Drexel Ames—that's it."

"Thanks old man. . . . Say, what are you going to make the lead?"

McLane put down his pencil. "Were you unconscious?"

Goose grinned. "Pretty near it. I was sampling the Seventy-five. Help me out, will you, McLane? Remember the Dreyfus story I wrote for you—"

McLane groaned. "Every time I get a good story exclusive some drunk who saved my skin sometime back in the eighties when I was soused comes whining to be saved. Aw, go and sit down. I'll write your goddam lead."

"Thanks, McLane. You're a good scout."

Goose took a comfortable seat in the lobby, and waited while his friend and savior wrote both stories and put them on the wire.

From time to time he fingered a small thick package in his right hand trousers' pocket. He was wondering how soon he could leave and go in search of a private telephone booth. Also if he could make the night air mail to New York.

It was nearly three o'clock before Goose reached his room in the Breakers.

He was weary, but he was happy.

He had played a hunch, taken a long chance, and it had worked.

Acting on impulse, impelled by the growing certainty that somewhere he had seen Allie Fitz-Hamon in convict garb, he had dashed to Helen Ilderton's office under cover of the darkness caused by the short circuit, and taken the souvenir photographs and finger-prints.

It had been a long chance. The lights might have come on any moment. He might have bumped into Helen in the office. Someone—one of the numerous dicks stationed about—might have stopped him on the way out.

But none of those things had happened. He had groped his way to the office, lit a match and found the precious package, slipped it into his pocket, and strolled through the garden, nonchalantly smoking a cigarette. Once on the Lake Trail, out of sight, he had quickened his pace, and while running to a safe place to telephone, had met up with McLane, and learned what had happened in the ballroom while he was at his own none too honorable business in the office.

Yes, he had been lucky—even to getting the story of the robbery on the wire, and saving his skin with the paper. He shuddered when he thought of the reception his telephone call charges reversed would have had, had he missed the news of the robbery. Cold perspiration broke out on his brow.

As it was, he was sitting pretty. He had—thanks to McLane—a fine story on the jewel theft. He had had a highly satisfactory conversation with George Clark, his new managing editor, and he had the package of photographs and thumb-prints in the night airmail.

He hoped it wouldn't be too hard on Helen. She was a nice kid. He hadn't treated her very well. But he'd make it up to her. It was also rather tough on the local police who could have put the complete file of finger-prints to good use. But if they were any good at all they could manage without them, and this was his one chance to settle his suspicion about Allie, and have it settled once and forever.

If Allie, under any alias, had ever been in the pen, his paper and the New York police would know in twenty-four hours. George Clark was all for pinning something on a nationally known figure like Allie and breaking the best Palm Beach scandal in seven years. If there was a thing in the world against Allie they'd find it, and spread it all over the world.

Goose had never before cared for tabloid papers, but now he took keen delight in picturing just the way George Clark would emblazon the tidings.

And if there was nothing on Allie, they'd have the pictures to run in the magazine section with a good "Society-Plays-Thief, — While-Real-Thief-Picks-Pockets" line, and he'd lay off Allie forever. He'd congratulate Marjorie on getting a sure enough, dyed-in-the-wool peer, and he'd spend two weeks' salary on a wedding present.

With this last not-so-pleasant thought, he prepared for bed. He was tired. Tireder than he had thought. So tired he'd treat himself to a good sleep for once.

In his pajamas he padded to the door and hung the "Do Not Disturb" sign outside. Left word with the night clerk not to call him before noon.

Then he crawled into bed, and was immediately asleep.

## CHAPTER IX

FOUR hours later, dreaming that he was waiting at the altar for Marjorie, who was walking down the aisle to him with Fitz-Hamon, who seemed to be her father, Goose woke with a start.

Someone was pounding and shouting vociferously at the door.

"Lemme in. Lemme in!" cried the well-known voice of Josh Huntington.

Furious at being aroused so soon from his slumbers, Goose stumbled to the door, unlocked it, and tumbled back into his bed. He was pulling the covers back over his ears when Josh, attired in a soft boiled shirt, and a melted winged collar, lunged into the room.

"Jumping Jehoshaphat! What a night. I want you to get Murphy, that piefaced flat-footed bum detective, fired off the force. And I want you to pin the dirtiest scandal in Palm Beach history on Charles Hamilton Gibbons. I don't care whether it's true or not. Get your dirty tabloid to think up something rotten and I'll pay. I'll pay any libel suit

Gibbons brings. I'll pay anything." And, as an after-thought, "If it takes my last cent I'll pay."

Reluctantly Goose sat up in bed, rubbed his eyes. "Didn't you see the sign on the door? I'm trying to sleep."

"Sleep! I've had none at all. I've been in the Main Street hoosegow all night, and it was a real Palm Beach Main Street and a real jail and no party."

Goose was wide awake now. "Say it again and say it slow." He was thinking what a swell yarn this would be. God was too good. Josh Huntington, oil magnate, in a Palm Beach hoosegow, suspected by Charles Hamilton Gibbons, one time competitor in the harness business back in Topeka, Kansas, of participation in a jewel robbery!

But Josh again rudely interrupted his calculations. Nor was Josh yet quite sober.

"There was I," he began heatedly, "looking for the butler's pantry because the tight-fisted old hypocrite had forgotten to feed us. I was just on the track of it when the lights went out. Fumbling in my pants pocket for a match when another door swung open and a fellow almost knocked me down. I took one look at him, and nearly dropped dead. It was the same guy that swiped my pile at Bradley's. The same guy in the rum runners' boat that almost drowned us at the Puritan.

"Maybe I'd had a drop too much. I made a lunge for him and he gives me a poke in the stomach and goes out the window. I was just going out after him and I would have caught him, when that bum detective named Murphy makes a flying tackle for my foot and begins to blow his whistle like he's lost his mind.

"Right away a whole mess of fellows come running, and that old addlebrained fool Gibbons. And instead of telling them to let me up, even if he didn't like me, he begins a cock-and-bull story about me being an accomplice in a jewel robbery going on in the parlor!"

Josh sat down and wiped his brow.

Goose was already out of bed, and dressing fast.

"Why don't you crawl in here, and get a few winks, Josh?"

"Thanks, I think I will. You're going to get *my* story into print?"

Goose grinned. "And how!"

"Good boy," Josh was easing himself into bed. Soon his snores, rhythmical and regular, rose on the quiet morning air.

Reporters and cameramen swarmed around the Duke suite at the Breakers. Mrs. Vincent Duke, pale but determined, received them in a body. She told the history and the value of the Duke necklace. She refused to say one word about her daughter's engagement to Lord Allan Fitz-Hamon. "You must realize that this is all very painful to us. We wish to avoid publicity," she said, enunciating each word clearly so that these rough-looking persons could understand. And then she passed around photographs of Marjorie, in her coming-out gown, the Duke necklace around her slender neck.

The reporters took the photographs and departed. For a few days the papers were full of it. As Marjorie was the only attractive young woman who was robbed, her pictures were featured. Mrs. Anthony Drexel Ames and her Cabochon ruby and broken leg took second place. Photographs of the Gibbons' mansion, fanciful drawings of the gang working in coatrooms and dim verandas vied with artists' conceptions of Josh Huntington languishing in the Palm Beach jail. There were long stories about Marjorie and Lord Allan Fitz-Hamon. Stories of the ancient enmity between Josh and Gibbons.

But jewel robberies at smart gatherings are not

uncommon. The whole thing would have dropped out of the papers in a week had not Ivy Brown suddenly come out of seclusion at her suite at the Alba, and announced that a diamond and pearl encrusted vanity case, left in the pocket of her evening wrap, had also been stolen, the night of the Gibbons' ball.

That revived the story. Pictures of Ivy, Ivy in formal evening costume, Ivy in lounging pajamas, Ivy in the briefest of brief yellow bathing suits, Ivy in the Burmese headdress she had worn in the Scandals, were broadcast all over the country.

All of this was hard on Marjorie. At a time when she wanted nothing more than to be left to dream of her love for Allie, to see him alone, and to further the romance that was all the world to her now, she was forced to see police inspectors, dodge nosey reporters, and listen to long harangues from her mother.

Mrs. Duke's health—always good in times of excitement—was perfect now. But she talked incessantly, sent wire after wire to her husband in New York, engaged in more long, unsatisfactory telephone conversations with him.

Vincent Duke was furious with the trend Marjorie's Palm Beach season had taken. He hated the publicity she was getting. Hoped she wasn't serious about wanting to become Lady Fitz-Hamon.

"No, I'm not prejudiced," he told his wife, over the telephone. "Or if I am, I'll put that aside. It is true that I don't want Marjorie to marry a foreigner. An American ought to be good enough for her. I don't want my money spent to bolster up some crumbling castle. I don't want to be laughed at for a sucker.

"But that's nothing. Nothing at all. It's Marjorie's happiness I'm thinking of. I tell you I don't believe there will be any happiness for the girl in an international marriage. There never seems to be.

"I've seen too much of it. She'll be looked upon as an outsider, an American, by Fitz-Hamon and his people. She'll be a Britisher to her own friends here. She'll never fit in anywhere.

"She hasn't been raised for that sort of thing. When she finds that he isn't faithful to her—don't interrupt me, I'm talking now!—her poor little heart will be broken.

"Then she will stick it out for two years or ten years or as long as she can endure it rather than admit she's made a mistake. I know Marjorie.

"And in the end, after I've spent enough to pay off the national debt, and all the Fitz-Hamons even to the third and fourth generation twice removed, have filled their flat pockets with good American money, Marjorie will come home.

"She'll come home, and I know exactly the way she'll look. I've seen plenty of them. She'll be thinner and harder. Her voice will be different. She'll laugh a great deal and all the genuine fun will be gone out of her. Maybe she will have a couple of children that she'll have to leave behind.

"Don't try to talk me into an international marriage, Alice! I know that girl better than you do. It just won't work."

All of which was hard on Mrs. Duke. With Allie on the point of a declaration, and Marjorie head over heels in love, and getting more publicity than any other débutante of the season, it was just like Vincent to take a stand like that.

Just as if she hadn't been through enough, having to chaperon Marjorie the night of the ball, while policemen sprayed stuff on her neck and tried to get finger-prints of the person who had snatched the necklace.

There wasn't a day that some inspector didn't come to question her and Marjorie again. Marjorie was beginning to look peaked, and though Allie wanted to take them on a quiet little trip in

Colonel Roget's houseboat which had been lent to him for a few weeks, they couldn't go until the miserable police investigation was finished.

It seems that there was some trouble about Mrs. Harry Brown. Mrs. Gibbons made a statement to the effect that she had not been invited to the ball. Mr. Gibbons, ignorant of his wife's stand, had said that she was. Two of the yellower journals hinted at a divorce, with the beautiful Ivy as co-respondent.

After a great fuss the police had a collection of finger-prints. A maid, two footmen and a waiter hired from the catering company for the occasion were under suspicion. But the man who left the print of thumb and forefinger on Marjorie's neck had not been apprehended.

Josh Huntington told his sensational story of recognizing the short, heavy-set man who cheated him out of three hundred dollars worth of chips at Bradley's, and almost swamped him in a rum runner's boat when his launch was leaving the Puritan.

Ivy who had been with him on both occasions flatly repudiated his story.

"I'd know the man at Bradley's if I saw him again," she said in a sworn statement to police inspectors, "but I would also swear that he did not take Mr. Huntington's money. Mr. Huntington had been drinking, and he was mistaken.

"Mr. Huntington had also been drinking heavily at the Puritan. He thought it was the same man, but it wasn't."

Goose hung around police headquarters in West Palm Beach. He had his own good reason for being anxious. He was waiting until the finger-prints they had got at the scene of the robbery were struck off, and broadcast to police throughout the country.

Not a word had he received from his own private investigations about Allie though he was urged from time to time by George Clark to send Palm Beach police findings without delay.

Finally the day arrived when the facsimiles were ready. Goose put his copies in the airmail with a sigh of thanksgiving.

Just time to reach the Gulf Stream Club, twenty miles below the Palm Beaches, to get the final chucker of the Cuban American finals.

The usual smart crowd was assembled. Women, perched on the back of open cars, held bright colored parasols, to protect themselves from the blazing sun. Their escorts, jauntily attired in riding breeches and sweaters, stood on the running-boards with field glasses, following every play of the competing teams.

It was a tie score with barely three minutes left to go, and excitement was intense. Goose had forgotten his enclosure pass, so he stood on the sidelines by the parked cars. A familiar voice attracted him, and he turned to see who it was. It was Shirley Swayne, and with her in the dark blue Minerva was Allie Fitz-Hamon. Shirley recognized him and waved. Allie returned Goose's greeting with his usual cold composure.

"I'm looking for Marjorie Duke. Have you seen her?" Goose asked, coming up to their car.

"I believe she's here somewhere. You'll probably find her in the thick of the cameramen," Shirley smiled.

Goose's eyes met Allie's. Allie's were expressionless. He appeared not to have heard. There were times when Goose admired the British. "Thanks, I'll look for her," he said.

He found her further down the line, in an open car with Mazie-Beth Lawrence.

Mazie-Beth promptly invited him to join them and Henry at the Oasis, when the match was over. "Henry has a guest card, so we might as well use it. It's awfully hard to get in usually. You can drive over with us, can't you?"

Goose accepted gratefully, just as the crowd sent up a mighty cheer, and the game was over.

He squeezed into the chummy roadster with the girls.

"Mind if I put my arm back of the seat?" he asked Marjorie, who was next to him.

"Why should she?" Mazie-Beth at the wheel, answered. "Her boy friend wouldn't mind. He was at the game with Shirley Swayne, and I think it's a shame."

"Mazie-Beth, you know I don't mind. Allie explained to me. And they are such old friends!"

"Well, I know what I'd do to Henry if I found him with Shirley Swayne!"

"Oh no, Mazie-Beth!"

Involuntarily Goose's arm tightened around Marjorie. He gave her a sympathetic little squeeze.

"I don't mind, really, I'm awfully sensible about those things," she said, looking up at him with wide, misty eyes.

Again Goose prayed that his hunch wouldn't be wrong. He even wished Fitz-Hamon luck with Shirley Swayne. It would make the break easier for Marjorie.

By one of those strange coincidences that seem to pursue people who want to avoid each other, Marjorie and Fitz-Hamon had chosen the same place for tea, and the bowing waiter, still further aiding fate, placed them at almost adjoining tables.

Henry, after an afternoon devoted principally to Martinis, was in fine form. He had a monocle someone had given him and was happily imitating the British, trying to keep the glass in his eye.

When he caught sight of Allie and the exotic Shirley he was all interest. "That's the girl he's engaged to," he whispered, pointedly nudging the girls. "I heard all about it in the locker room this afternoon. She keeps him. Can you beat that?"

Mazie-Beth could have killed him. "Henry, it isn't true. And I wish you'd be more careful what you say. Lord Allan is Marjorie's fiancé."

Henry's face turned a slow and painful scarlet. "Oh! I always get everything wrong. Mazie-Beth will tell you I always do, Marjorie. I beg your pardon. I'm sure I was mistaken."

Goose's hand closed over Marjorie's under the tablecloth. He felt it trembling in his, but she managed a smile, said, "It's all right, Henry—people say things. I don't mind."

A moment later someone asked Shirley to dance, and Allie came immediately to their table. "Will you dance with me, Marjorie?"

She rose, and Henry looked after their departing figures with ill-concealed wonder.

"It beats me," he said, turning to Goose, "the way women fall for men like that."

Goose beamed. He took an immediate liking to Henry. He saw that he had far greater perception than he was usually credited with.

"The very thing I've pondered on, myself."

"And they say that women are worse gossips than men!" Mazie-Beth cried. "Why *I'd* be ashamed to believe all those tales they tell about him and Shirley Swayne—"

"And Ivy Brown and Mimi De Vaux, and Sunshine Johnson—" Goose couldn't resist adding.

"I hate to see Marjorie throw herself away on a blighter like that," Henry broke in earnestly, readjusting the monocle.

"Yes, you'd rather see her marry somebody like you!" Mazie-Beth finished bitterly.

The dance was over. With a bow and a few whispered words, Allie left Marjorie to return to his own table.

She sat down, all happy and excited. "Mazie-Beth! He wants you and Henry for the fishing trip on the houseboat as soon as that hateful police business is over. Isn't that wonderful?"

## CHAPTER X

IN Shirley Swayne's apartment at the Royal Poinciana a strictly business conversation was going on.

"I don't care in the least if you want to marry that Duke girl," Shirley said, laying down her pink enamelled hairbrush, and turning a serious face to her late admirer. "You can do just as you like. Only, get this, Allie—I'm not responsible for your bills once you leave my bed and board. Make up your mind, pretty boy!"

"Marriage means nothing to me," Allie said guardedly.

"No? Then why couldn't we have been married, long ago?"

"Shirley—I've explained about that. You know how my family felt about my first marriage. Because Flora was in the Follies—"

"I'm not in the Follies. I'm the Vicomtesse de l'Inois."

"I know, but you know as well as I do—"

"That I'm not good enough for you!"

"No, no—Shirley, don't fly into a temper. Be patient—be—"

"I'm sick of being patient. While I've been patient you've got yourself engaged to Marjorie Duke, and you've been carrying on with that disgusting Ivy Brown. That's what bothers me the most. I knew Ivy back in Chicago in 1918 and she was living with a cheap sport called Dutch Louie. How do you like taking a tin-horn gambler's leavings?"

"If you're going to be vulgar, I'm going."

"Go ahead!" She sounded final.

He made a step or two toward the door. Opened his gold mounted cigarette case, drew out a cigarette. Very slowly he lit it, watching Shirley all the time. She made no move.

"Shirley, I can't do it! You know you mean everything in the world to me!"

He threw the cigarette aside. Came and took her in his arms.

Long and furiously Ivy Brown called Allie FitzHamon's room at the Royal Poinciana.

Small Negro boys wandered through lobby and grill chanting, "Lo'd Fump-Hump, Lo'd Fump-Hump!"

Lord Fitz-Hamon was somewhere about the hotel, the clerk thought, but he could not be found. Would madam leave a message?

"No!"

Ivy wept as she packed, with the aid of a curious, slightly frightened hotel maid. Her tears fell on maize satin negligées, black georgette stepins, yellow and white silk sports dresses and evening gowns of pale gold tissue. "Never mind folding!" she scolded. "Just throw everything in. Didn't I tell you I was in a hurry?"

"Yas'm."

"Well, then, hurry! Don't you see *I'm* hurrying?" But when her clothes were in the trunks, and there was nothing to do but slip small personal things into the open dressing case Ivy ceased hurrying.

Slowly, one by one, she dropped in powder box, handkerchief bag, the gold-back brushes from her dresser.

Once more she paused to read the brief note that was the cause of her going. It was from Allie Fitz-Hamon. It advised her to get the first fast train North. Stated that her mother in Toronto was failing and she had better waste no time in reaching her bedside.

Ivy wept again as she re-read the note. Her tears were not for her mother, that lady having been dead for nearly twenty years. Her tears were for her husband, and it must be admitted for herself.

Allie's note meant more than it said. It meant that her relationship to Louis Brown—known in certain circles as Dutch Louie—was either known, or about to be.

It meant that Louie himself was in trouble. It meant that Allie Fitz-Hamon was looking after her for old time's sake, and that was all. He was warning her to leave Palm Beach before it was too late. And he wasn't making the least effort to see her, to bid her good-bye, to do any one of the small, comforting things he could have done.

"Just like a man!" Ivy sobbed, pushing the nervous maid aside, and shutting the last bag herself. "Selfish hog! If I get out of this I'll go settle down somewhere with Louie!"

She meant it. She forgot, womanlike, how many times she had promised herself the same thing.

Dutch Louie, though she didn't know it, had already settled down—settled down in the Chicago city jail. The finger-prints he left on Marjorie Duke's neck as he snatched her necklace under cover of the darkness at the Gibbons' Ball were his undoing.

Their facsimiles in the Prescott penitentiary, where he had recently served a year, established his identity as Louie Broune, alias Brown, alias Dutch Louie.

They caught him in a Chicago rooming house. The loot was never recovered, though the Insurance Companies kept the cases open for months.

Ivy—her identity traced through the guest lists which recorded the arrival of both Mr. and Mrs. Harry Brown—was taken off her train at Buffalo.

Her life romance with broken nosed, squatty little Dutch Louie was spread—with appropriate photographs—over every state in the Union, and eventually found its way into most of the American papers on the Continent. Certain American captains of industry who had devoted considerable time and trouble, and gone to great expense to win that golden beauty's heart, looked at the photographs of pig-eyed Dutch Louie, and shook their heads. They couldn't understand it.

There was nothing to connect Ivy with the jewel robbery. After a while they let her go. And so, instead of settling down with Louie, she went to Hollywood and settled down with a director, who used her recent publicity to the best possible advantage.

And long before then Palm Beach had forgotten the entire affair. That is, Palm Beach in general.

Erskine Gander, destined never to be long out of hot water, was not yet breathing easy. There was the matter of Helen Ilderton, for one thing.

Helen had left the Gibbons'—not without a more or less direct hint from Mrs. Charles Hamilton Gibbons—and was looking for a job.

It was up to Goose to get it for her. Like a lost puppy she followed him around, half bold, half timid, looking at him adoringly through thick, horn-rimmed glasses.

"I want to get into newspaper work," she told him, earnestly. "I've often felt that I could write. People have told me so, and I've had some practical experience. I was woman's editor of the *Aegis* at college, for two years."

Goose squirmed. He didn't know how to tell her that there wasn't a chance. "I'd hate to see you go into newspaper work," he said, instead. "You'd get hard boiled and—"

"No indeed. You don't know me, if you think that, Goose. I wouldn't let it affect me."

"Well, you'd meet a lot of hard-boiled customers—"

"No one could be worse than Mrs. Gibbons!"

"That's so," Goose pretended to agree. He scratched his head, uncertain of how he was going to get out of it. Why wouldn't the girl take a nice job with some other society dame, or maybe the Chamber of Commerce?

So to make up for his other failings he devoted all of his free time to her. In a way he enjoyed it. It was doing penance. Every time he sat down at a table with gawky, over-eager Helen Ilderton, and saw the exquisite Marjorie on Allie Fitz-Hamon's arm, he took morbid pleasure in his own suffering.

He made up a kind of game to play with himself. It was to see how many synonyms for "cad," "libertine" or "fop" he could think of while looking at Allie out of the corner of his eye and carrying on an animated conversation with Helen.

At times he thought Marjorie looked ill. She was always so gay, so tense and flushed with excitement. She seemed thinner, too, and there were times when her blue eyes were shadowed and tired.

"Why don't you try staying home and getting a good night's sleep sometime?" he asked her.

"Too many interesting things to do."

"With Allie!"

"Why not?" she flashed back at him.

He cursed himself for blundering. Now she would think him officious.

He made several other attempts to have a word with her one afternoon, but Allie was right at her elbow every minute, and as he was taking Helen around so much now, there was always the problem of what to do with her. Helen never seemed to know anyone. She just sat there, and waited for him to talk to her, or dance with her.

"My God," he thought, "if I don't get her a job before her money gives out, I suppose I'll have to marry her, and if I have to sit opposite to her three times a day for the rest of my life and have her ogle me through those horn-rimmed specs I'm liable to go nutty."

He was so preoccupied with his own affairs that he failed to come to any significant conclusions in regard to Shirley Swayne.

Even Mrs. Duke was beginning to worry about her. Allie was with Marjorie every minute, but everywhere they went Shirley was sure to appear sooner or later.

At Palm Beach you do meet the same people repeatedly, but this was getting beyond the bounds of probability. Lunching at Sea-Spray, or the Bath and Tennis Club, teaing at the Sea Horse, or dancing at the Embassy—no matter where they went, they'd see Shirley.

Sometimes she swept in alone. Took a table near them. Appeared to be waiting for someone. Sometimes she came in with a gay overdressed party. Sometimes with some distinguished escort or other.

Always her long, dark eyes were fastened on Marjorie and Allie with silent, sly amusement. Sometimes she said things—little sparkling asides to her companions. There would be laughter and then all the heads would turn carefully towards Marjorie and Allie.

Mrs. Duke began to dread going out. If only she didn't have to be civil to the Vicomtesse! If she only dared cut her, or see to it that others did! But Shirley Swayne's social position was if anything more secure than her own. She was accepted by those who were in a position to determine such things. But Mrs. Duke dreamed of dark, sloe-eyed Vicomtesses in her sleep. She fell into a nervous habit of watching doors for Shirley to make her regal entrance.

Shirley always made entrances. She strolled into

tearooms, laughing and chatting, sometimes swinging her immense, fine straw hat in her hand. She swept into ballrooms. She had a little trick of hesitating just inside the door, then making a little rush for some dowager or gray-haired aristocrat, both beautiful hands outstretched, her thin face lit with amazed joy.

"Madame Semour . . . ah . . . to find you here!" Or "Colonel Roget . . . now I *am* glad!"

And it was just a matter of time before she'd see Allie, and the Dukes. A smiling greeting for the women—a slow, meaning look in Allie's direction, a slight gesture of her long, graceful arm.

Allie would have to murmur excuses, make his way to her. She never kept him long. She would rattle off two or three sentences—often in French—lean back, smile up at him amusedly. Then another slow, amused smile in the direction of the Dukes, who were trying to be natural and nonchalant on the other side of the room. Sometimes she gave Allie a playful push. Always she made it evident that she was sending him back to Marjorie.

Marjorie smarted with embarrassment. Mrs. Duke tried in vain to sneer at the ex-movie actress's bad manners. She could find nothing to say. Shirley Swayne's savoir-faire exceeded her own. Her gowns were as exquisite, her jewels, the few, rather bizarre pieces she wore, almost priceless. And since Mrs. Duke's daughter was about to marry the Vicomtesse's old admirer, she could hardly malign the latter's reputation.

There were times, though, when Marjorie could hardly bear it. If she had had someone to talk to it would have helped. She made ineffectual efforts to write Mid Bennett. But that wouldn't do. It was against this sort of thing that Mid's mother had warned her when her coming-out party was being arranged.

"You're too young to know men," the horsey Isabelle Bennett had told her. "You'll either marry some rich young boy and have to be brought up—the pair of you—by a nursery governess, or it will be some much older man of the world and you'll have to face his ex-wives or ex-mistresses later."

Marjorie remembered, with a twisted little smile, how she had once told Erskine Gander that she didn't mind about Allie's affairs.

She had thought she didn't. But that was before Shirley Swayne started following them around, and being possessive. She did mind now—terribly.

The part that she minded most was Shirley's being right there all the time. It was one thing to think of the glamorous Shirley and a distant, romantic—even wicked—affair. It was rather thrilling to think of marrying a man who had had affairs with women like Shirley Swayne. It didn't matter that Allie wasn't good. Marjorie knew so little about life that she could placidly accept situations that a less sheltered girl would shrink from.

But it wasn't easy to fit Shirley—Shirley right on the scene, Shirley with an arm through Allie's at the polo match, Shirley signalling him to come to her at a dinner-dance—into the past.

Shirley was all too much of the present.

And Shirley was laughing at her—was handing Allie over to her with a "You may have him for a while" gesture that was just too much.

Goose might have helped. He had been more comforting, more understanding, than any one of the busy, smart people she had met at Palm Beach. But Goose was all wrapped up in that tall skinny social secretary now. When she telephoned his room, timidly asking for Mr. Gander, the clerk always said he was out, and she never left a message. She was too self-conscious for that, too uncertain of herself.

And about this time she began to receive anonymous letters.

## CHAPTER XI

ANONYMOUS letters, or rather anonymous marked newspaper clippings, are much more common in smart circles than one likes to admit. The ambitious send flattering newspaper notices about themselves to those whom they wish to impress. The spiteful clip notices of their "friends'" ex-wives or husbands, or successful rivals, and see that they get a wide circulation. The plain envelope with its bit of clipped print inside is a familiar part of the morning mail.

But it was all new to Marjorie Duke, and she suffered.

Hardly a day went by that she didn't receive some line about Lord Fitz-Hamon and Shirley Swayne. Most of the clippings were from the scandal sheets. Some were torn from the more respectable papers, and were nothing more than photographs of Shirley.

To make matters worse, her mother was ill. The business of marrying Marjorie to a title had proved more arduous than Alice Duke had anticipated.

Specialists resumed their interrupted visits, husky Swedish masseuses were sent for, dark skinned, white turbaned Swamis were once more a part of the Duke ménage.

For years Mrs. Duke had been using poor health as an excuse for indolence, and thwarted ambition. Now that her lifelong ambition was about to be realized, and she needed strength, it failed her. Try as she might, she could no longer drag herself from place to place to chaperon Marjorie. Mazie-Beth Lawrence was seized upon to do duty in her stead, bribed with presents, coaxed and nagged into prolonging her stay at Palm Beach.

From her pillows the invalid directed operations. Chose Marjorie's gowns, issued innumerable directions, asked questions.

Marjorie's nerves were frayed, too. She was tired, and homesick. Homesick for someone to talk to, someone who'd really care what happened to her.

Once she met Erskine Gander in the lobby, and pulled him over to a chintz-covered Chesterfield.

"Talk to me," she begged. "Say something funny. Mother's ill, and Mazie-Beth wants to go back to California—and I'm so tired—"

He took her two small hands in his. "Marj—you aren't happy!"

She tried to blink back the tears. Childishly, her lip trembled and she bit it. "Oh yes, I'm happy." She withdrew her hands from his, and began to search for a handkerchief.

Goose tried again. "You aren't wearing the Fitz-Hamon ring yet. Everything all right?"

"Yes. We're practically engaged. Allie has to hear from his father, and he wants to see my father, too. It's quite hard to marry into the British nobility, Goose. You have to have settlements, and all sorts of things—"

"So I've heard," dryly—from Goose.

"So much fuss—" Marjorie quavered, "and—and—" She was going to add: "Shirley Swayne is so hateful!"—but she couldn't say that—not even to Goose.

"Look here, Marj—why do you do this now? You're just a kid. Next year I'll bet you meet somebody better than Allie—"

A muffled, "No—no—"

"I mean an earl, or a prince. Or maybe some good old American boy. There must be somebody you could love."

"No—there's nobody—"

Goose edged closer. His face was all alight.

"Marjorie, honey, you aren't in love with Fitz-Hamon."

"I don't know—I don't know anything any more."

"I know you aren't. Marjorie, you're too young to make a marriage like that—just for show. What does it matter who you marry if you're happy, honey?"

Marjorie sat up, opened her powder box, began to powder her straight little nose. "Goose, you'll just make me more unsettled. I ought to be ashamed of myself, giving in that way. It isn't fair to Allie."

"Oh, damn Allie!"

"Please don't, Goose. When you say things like that you just hurt me. You don't understand. You've got one kind of life to lead, and I've got another. I—I want to be successful in my kind of life. I want to marry in my first season. I don't want to be left over."

"You don't have to be left over. I'll marry you, Marj, and I won't make you wait while I ask my papa and mama either!"

Marjorie laughed. "Goose, you darling! I believe you would! And then what would poor Miss What's-her-name do? But you'd better be careful.

Some day this weakness of offering to marry every girl you meet is going to get you in trouble. Some girl is going to accept you!"

"Not much danger!"

They parted in a gale of laughter. But two minutes later Goose's brow was corrugated. It was none of his business of course, but something ought to be done. The blighter was all right, of course. His hunch at the Gibbons' Ball had been all wrong. If there was anything wrong with Fitz-Hamon the tabloid would have had the dope on him before this. And if Marjorie's people didn't object to Allie's women it certainly wasn't up to him to say anything more.

"But it's a damn shame, just the same!" he thought, slamming on his hat, and preparing to go out in search of news on Rum Runners' Row.

Marjorie's merriment didn't last much longer than Goose's. She dreaded going back to the suite, and having to meet a barrage of questions from her mother. . . . "Who was at the Bath and Tennis Club? . . . What did Evelyn Throckmarten have on? . . . Did Allie say anything about where you'd live after your marriage? . . . What did you have for lunch? Were the Varneys there? . . . Was Shirley Swayne there?"

Marjorie knew what the questions would be in advance. And Shirley *had* been there. She was all alone, sunning herself on the sand. Her blue-black hair was brushed back from her face in a plain, boyish swirl. Her bathing suit was black jersey, cut to her waistline in back. Her long, sun-tanned, sinuous body was brown against the white sand. She napped like a great, beautiful cat in the strong sunlight. Every time Marjorie looked at her, her eyes were closed, long, heavily mascaraed lashes shadowing her tanned cheek, and yet Marjorie felt that she was watching . . . watching every move that she and Allie made. . . .

Now that she was used to Allie she no longer found him so thrilling. There were times when conversation was difficult, when they sat in uncomfortable silence, with nothing to say to each other . . . and Shirley Swayne's red lips curled into a slow, amused smile. . . . "Enjoy yourselves if you can," she seemed to be saying wordlessly, and laughing at them, because they couldn't. . . .

Poor Marjorie! She looked so young and carefree and pretty. She felt so old, and worn, and plain, sometimes. And for all her rose damask bedroom, boudoir and bath, and the big, cool sitting room of the Duke suite, she had nowhere to go—

nowhere she could escape the watchful eye of her mother. Nowhere she could be alone—to think things out for herself.

So she decided to stay in the lobby a while longer, and write a letter to her father.

When she was very little, she and Vincent Duke had been playfellows. They had roughhoused up and down stairs and played hide-and-go-seek in the halls of the big brownstone house in New York.

Once, while her mother was at Biarritz, he had taken her and her indignant nurse on a shooting trip to Canada. There would have been more of such trips, more companionship between them, but Mrs. Duke refused to have her only child made into a tomboy.

So Marjorie was sent from one school to another, "making the right contacts, forming the right friendships." Vincent Duke buried himself more and more in business. Now there was still affection, but an odd restraint, between them.

Marjorie chewed her pen. She didn't know just where to begin. At last she wrote:

Dear Father:

Mother seems a little better today, and Dr. Black says that it is nothing serious. But I think that this

Palm Beach season has been too hard on her. I am tired out too, and shall be glad when we join you again.

Couldn't you get away for a little while? I could go with you to Nassau or somewhere, if Mother did not want to go. Please do, Father. I will be a grown-up married woman soon, and maybe we won't ever be able to go anywhere together again.

Mother says that you have agreed to my marrying Allie Fitz-Hamon. I hope you will like him. Mother says he is the best English type.

Father, I mean it about going away somewhere with you! We could leave here any time, because I am engaged, and it can be announced from one place as well as another. I could come home right away if you wanted. I have accepted an invitation to go on Allie's house party on the *Nautilus* Saturday, but Mother won't be able to go and Mazie-Beth and Henry Lawrence, who are to chaperon me, don't care to go really, so I could get out of it, in case you want to go somewhere with me.

Of course if you do not want to, I can stay here. It is a very beautiful place, and I am having a very gay time.

Only if you would like to go somewhere, Father, I could get away.

My love,

MARJORIE.

With the letter in the mail, she felt better. She went upstairs to face her mother and the questions.

Mrs. Duke was lying in bed, propped in a nest of satin and filet pillows.

"Allie has been here."

"Allie! Why I just left him a little while ago. What did he want?"

"Oh nothing. That is, nothing that would interest you."

"I'm supposed to be engaged to him," Marjorie said mildly. "I should think that almost anything about Allie would be considered of interest to me."

Mrs. Duke looked offended. "Purely a business matter. Don't worry me with your questions, Marjorie. If you're going to be happily married you must learn not to ask too much about your husband."

Marjorie pulled at the folds of her dress.

Mrs. Duke relaxed again. The worry gradually erased itself from her pale eyes. Her pleased self-satisfaction came back.

"You don't know how fortunate you are. Many girls would like to be in your place."

"I know, Mother."

"Sometimes I think you don't realize what this means, my dear. To be quite frank, a titled match is more than I dared hope for. Titles, you know, don't grow on trees. Lord Fitz-Hamon comes from one of the oldest families in England."

"But his first wife was in the Follies," Marjorie said bitterly.

"Don't be cynical. It isn't your type. Leave that to Evelyn Throckmarten! . . . Of course his first wife was in the Follies. Young men of Allie's type frequently marry beneath them the first time. That is why it is so much more important to be chosen for a second, serious marriage."

"Yes, I suppose so."

"Marjorie, I don't understand you. I wish you wouldn't look so abused. Now, Marjorie Duke, don't tell me that you are letting this Shirley Swayne affair upset you."

"Perhaps—"

"I'm surprised at you. I expected more of you than that. Oh, Marjorie. If you're going to make trouble for me now—after all my work and sacrifice—"

Marjorie studied her slim, ringless fingers.

"I don't know, Mother. I'm blue. That's all. I—I don't want to marry Allie as much as I did—"

"Marjorie!"

"I can't help it—I don't—"

"Marjorie! You can't do it—not now—it's too late."

"It's not too late. It isn't announced. I don't want to be married. I want to go home. . . . Oh, Mother, I can't help it—I don't want to. . . . I'm afraid of Shirley Swayne. She laughs at me. I—"

Marjorie was crying now. Painful, heartbroken sobs.

Mrs. Duke was beside herself. Her head ached; she felt sick and miserable; she'd worked so hard. . . . And here was Marjorie—spoiling everything.

"Try to control yourself, Marjorie, please. Really, you are being too childish."

"I can't help it. I've felt this way for days, only I didn't d-dare say it, and now I have and—"

"Please, my dear—please!"

"Mother, I'm afraid!"

"Nonsense! This is just nerves. It's nothing. Promise me you'll say nothing to Allie until—"

"But my mind is made up. I know—"

"You'll break my heart!"

"What about mine?"

"Yours was going to be broken if you didn't get Allie two weeks ago. You're just a child. It doesn't matter whether you think you love Allie now or not. You will later. You will have a beautiful life with him. Everyone will envy you. Think of your lovely home in London, and the country place in Wales. All that will be yours some day, when Allie's father and uncle die. Think of that." Mrs. Duke, thoroughly frightened herself now, was soothing Marjorie as she would a fretful child.

The tears had stopped. Marjorie, more than a little ashamed of her show of emotion, wiped her eyes, said in a voice that she tried hard to keep steady, "All right. I won't say anything. Only let's not go on the house party. I couldn't stand Shirley Swayne for a whole week-end. I really couldn't."

"But you must. I've assured Allie—"

Marjorie gave up. When her mother's voice broke, quavered pitifully, was choked with tears, she could not hold out against her. And, moreover, she realized that Shirley Swayne's inclusion on this house party was just as bitter a blow to her mother as to herself. Mrs. Duke had not dared to oppose it. There never had been anything definitely against the Vicomtesse. She had always been clever enough to be discreet. And to take the scandals of the tabloids seriously would mean cutting out half the social register. . . . The engagement, after all, was not announced, and at this stage of the game Mrs.

Duke could not come into open conflict with Allie. And, besides, it would have put her and Marjorie in a ridiculous position. It was much the best to assume that everything was as it should be between Lord Fitz-Hamon and the Vicomtesse de l'Inois.

Marjorie stooped and kissed the grayish mottled cheek resting against pink satin cushions.

"I'll go," she promised.

Mrs. Duke wept with relief. She was not a brave woman. The thought of what might happen if Marjorie failed her now filled her with panic.

She had lent Allan Fitz-Hamon seventeen thousand dollars. He was to return it to her within five days.

If Vincent found that out . . . Alice Duke winced as she remembered the scene he had made when he found she had paid ten thousand francs to a gigolo in Paris. . . . "Throw your money in the Seine—buy anything you want—but don't ever let me hear of your spending any more money on men!" he had stormed.

This was different. Besides she'd have it back before Vincent could find it out—unless Marjorie ruined everything. . . .

Alice Duke sank back on her pillows. Did ever woman work harder and get less thanks?

## CHAPTER XII

IT was Saturday morning, and the Duke suite at the Breakers was charged with excitement. Belated packages from shops where Marjorie had made last minute purchases were still arriving. Dusky bellhops tapped, returned garments left to be pressed. Tissue paper and lingerie were scattered in delicate disarray all over the bed. One maid packed, the other helped Marjorie dress.

In the adjoining bedroom Mrs. Duke lay back on her pillows, in a state verging on collapse. She had had a horrible night.

Vincent Duke, on the long distance telephone from New York, had aroused her sometime after midnight. It seemed that Marjorie had written him a childish letter which he interpreted to be a plea for help. Some silly thing Marjorie had said had made him think she was unhappy and wanted to return to New York.

"But, Vincent, you don't *understand!*" she had wailed.

"I understand too damn well. You bring that girl home, or I'll come there and get her!"

"You'll do no such thing!"

He had hung up then—his temper triumphing as usual. Alice Duke glanced at the rose leather traveling clock at her bedside table. Never had hands crawled so slowly. She wouldn't draw a comfortable breath until Marjorie was gone, and the *Nautilus* well out to sea. It wasn't like Vincent to make idle threats. . . . Would those girls never finish? Wasn't it time for Allie to arrive? She had sent Godfrey in the Minerva to the Alba for Allie and his bags. (It was inconvenient, but if she didn't do it Shirley Swayne would take him in her car, and that would start everything wrong.)

"Oh, if I could only go myself," Mrs. Duke thought wildly. "If I just had my health! Marjorie is so childish. What chance will she have against that Swayne woman? If only the engagement were announced, then I wouldn't worry. And Mazie-Beth's no help. She means well enough, but she's too selfish. . . . Dear, dear . . . I wish it were all over!"

Marjorie, waiting expectant and uneasy for the ring that would announce Allie Fitz-Hamon, wished the same thing.

But she seemed gay and happy, even if she wasn't. She embraced her mother when the summons came, told her not to worry, and hurried down to Allie, eyes bright, cheeks flushed with excitement.

The *Nautilus* was crawling along at a good six knots an hour. Large, unwieldy, slow moving, she housed ten guests and a crew of twelve.

The deck was broad and spacious; the cabins below, with their wide plate-glass windows—so different from the stuffy portholes on faster cruisers—were spacious and luxuriously appointed.

Because it was built for cruising on tropical seas there were no saloons. They ate, played cards, danced and lounged on the deck.

Marjorie was giddy with strange, half morbid excitement. She took a second "Southern Honeysuckle" from the tray the Filipino steward was passing, and linked her arm through Josh Huntington's. Thank God, Allie had been considerate enough to yield to her wishes and invite old Josh, in spite of the fact that he considered the retired oil magnate an old bore. "I'm the extra lady, you're the extra man. We'll have to console each other!" she whispered, laughing.

Josh took a hurried look toward the deckhouse, where Allie and Shirley, in huge leather chairs, were watching the quartermaster at the wheel, and chatting with Colonel Roget's skipper, a rosy-cheeked, serious little man from Key West. Shirley, since the boat left, had hardly left Allie's side.

"That's my baby in there, but she don't seem to know it. This is the damnedest managed house party I ever was on," Josh complained. "When you're Lady Fitz-Hamon arrange 'em differently, will you?"

"Indeed I will!"

"Craziest guest list I ever saw. You and Allie, and Shirley—she was supposed to be for me, think of it!—and I, and the Lawrences, and the Throckmarten girl and that sap John Browning, and then the two Evans girls. Why the Evans girls? Who are they meant for, the Hawaiian orchestra?"

Marjorie giggled. "I guess so. Josh, how many Southern Honeysuckles can you drink without getting tight?"

"I don't know, child, but I know you've had all your mother would want you to have." He took the thin green glass with its thick amber-colored content from her, and downed it himself.

"This isn't the life for you," he said, leaning back against the rail, and surveying her with speculating, half-closed eyes.

"You seem to like it, Josh!"

"Yes. It's good for me, child. I'm fifty-one years old, and my life is all lived. So I play the fool. I throw money away on fast blondes like Ivy Brown, and folks laugh at me. Oh, don't pretend, Marjorie—I know what they say about old Josh Huntington.

"But what does it matter if Ivy and her kind do play me for a sucker? I have more money than I'll ever be able to spend. I haven't a chick or child to leave it to. I haven't a dozen real friends in the world. Oh, one or two old fellows I kind of look out for, back in Oklahoma, one or two others scattered around—"

"Josh, everybody likes you!" ("Everybody except Allie," she was thinking.) Her warm hand curled into his. She meant it so sincerely.

He smiled a little bitterly. "There—if I were just twenty years younger I'd give your Allie a run for it. But I'm not. Marry him, if you love him, child, and go back home with him. Don't hang around these places—Palm Beach, White Sulphur, Nice, Monte Carlo—all that. Too many vultures flying around—too much blackmail, husband-stealing, scandal.

"Settle down in the English country with your

Allie, and get yourself a lot of horses and dogs, and a few old barnyard cats, and be happy with your babies."

"Awfully exciting!"

"Excitement's just relative, child. I had more excitement and more happiness when I was in the harness business, back in Topeka, and lived in a furnished cottage I paid $27.50 a month for, than I've ever had since. . . . Because I had a wife and baby I loved. . . . They're both gone now. . . . When they found oil on that little old piece of land I had out in Oklahoma Territory and I knew I was going to be a rich man, I sat down and I cried, Marjorie. I cried because it all came too late. My Bessie was gone . . . and the little fellow too. . . . I nearly went crazy thinking . . . about it. . . . But I'm not sorry now. I'm glad Bessie and I just had each other, and not a lot of money, and an artificial life. . . ."

"Josh, you ought to marry again," she said softly. "Why don't you? You could be happy again!"

He shook his head. . . . They stood at the rail, this elderly fat playboy who was seldom sober after five P.M., and inexperienced young Marjorie Duke, and held hands in broad daylight!

Josh's mood changed first. "If somebody doesn't do something about it, this party's going to be a halo. Let's dance. Hey you!" He shouted to the two Hawaiians, softly strumming in their corner. "Get hot! Give us some jazz. We want to shake a leg!"

The Evans girls, arm in arm, curly-headed and flapperish in hand-blocked brilliantly flowered linen lounging pajamas and white and scarlet sabots, came up from their stateroom and began to dance together, singing as they swayed to the languorous, lilting air.

John Browning, too unsteady to dance after an injudicious mixture of rye and soda and very ginny Stingray cocktails, with a few sips from Evelyn's Southern Honeysuckle, sat himself down to provide a hand-clapping accompaniment. Evelyn sat on his lap, her long white duck legs sprawled on the deck. She was wearing sailor's trousers over her low-backed purple bathing suit.

In a moment Henry Lawrence came on deck with Mazie-Beth, and Allie and Shirley joined them too. The dance was on. The Hawaiians mopped moist brows, threw themselves into the orgy of rhythm.

For an hour Marjorie was almost deliriously

happy. After that first dance with Shirley, Allie danced dance after dance with her, refusing to allow anyone to cut in. "I'm not going to let you get away," he whispered. "I have so little time with you, darling. Oh, for the day when we can cruise alone . . . no stupid crowd to bother us!"

Marjorie looked up into his handsome, earnest face. She thought of Josh—and what he had said. "Oh, Allie—if it will ever come true!"

"It *is* going to be true—and soon. Aren't you glad?"

She looked away. "I don't know, Allie. Right now I am . . . but sometimes—"

"Sometimes what, sweet?"

"Sometimes—I'm not so sure."

"Tut—schoolgirl qualms, my little Marjorie. Come, pour tea for me, won't you?"

One of the Filipino boys was carrying the tea-things. Another was spreading a lace cloth. A third brought a tray of tiny sandwiches, small iced cakes.

Marjorie's hand shook as she lifted the heavy silver teapot. Then she caught Shirley Swayne's critical eye. She banished the nervousness; Lady Fitz-Hamon wouldn't be made nervous by an ex-movie actress. . . .

Mazie-Beth congratulated her, afterwards. "You

have a lot of poise for a kid, Marj. You won't blink an eye when you're presented, and all that sort of thing. Now, it's entirely different with me. Mama had everything arranged for me, that summer we were in England, and I simply got cold feet. I just pictured myself getting tied up in my train and being unable to get up again after the curtsey. So I wouldn't do it. Mama was simply furious, and you can't blame her. . . . I wish I'd brought pajamas. Marj, you and I are the only women here in skirts!"

Marjorie looked down at her trimly pleated white piqué, and shook her head. "I think we look nicer than the others," she said stoutly. "Anyway, Allie doesn't like girls in trousers—I've heard him say so—and I think that Shirley Swayne's impersonation of a French sailor is just plain common!"

"But fetching," Mazie-Beth sighed. "She would do it, even to the gold hoops in her ears. Even Henry is intrigued. Oh, Hen! Hen! Come here! Henry, don't you like Shirley Swayne's costume? There, Marj, I told you he would."

"It suits her," Henry said judiciously. "One excuses a woman—particularly an actress—for the theatrical. But why is Allie Fitz-Hamon done up as a skipper? Pale blue yachting jacket with brass buttons, and that cap! I'd no more wear—"

"No, you haven't the figure for it, but Allie has, and he looks wonderful, darling. I only wish I could say the same for you. I pick you out the grandest sweaters, and think you're going to look like something in them, and then you look like just the same old meal sack!"

"But correct, my dear. Correct. Fitz-Hamon may be natty, but he's all wrong. Colonel Roget never gets himself up like that. It isn't proper."

The dancers on the other end of the deck had stopped to watch and wave to the guests on the *Aera,* a huge Diesel yacht, passing on the starboard side.

"It looks just like a yacht I saw once at Coronado, only that had two smokestacks," Mazie-Beth said. "I think ships look so much more dressy with lots of chimneys. The boat we went to England on last year had three!"

"Come, Mazie-Beth! Dance!" Henry took his wife in his arms. Over his shoulder he said to Marjorie, "All my wife's brains are in her feet!"

Allie's easy laugh joined Marjorie's. "Dance?"

"I'd love to!"

When the Hawaiians weakened, they turned on the Victrola. Even John Browning left the bar long enough to sober up a bit, and slide around.

"This crowd is jazz crazy," Josh panted, letting the youngest Evans sister drag him about the deck in her version of the Buck 'n' Wing for two.

When they were worn out at last they all went swimming in the warm waters of the Bay. All but Shirley Swayne who was afraid of the water. . . . "I never swim, it's such a bore," she explained.

Marjorie laughed to herself as her slim body cleaved through the limpid pale jade water. . . . So all Shirley's bathing at the Bath and Tennis and the Beach and Cycle was a pose! All she did was sun herself! Well, you might sun yourself there, but you had to know how to swim if you wanted to play in the water around a houseboat. They were cruising in the warm water of Biscayne Bay, well below Miami now.

After the swim there were more cocktails, and then dinner, and a long lazy evening on deck. Shirley, in a huff over something, went to her cabin early, so Josh consoled himself with the Evans girls, and one by one Marjorie's doubts vanished.

Allie was the old Allie again, the Allie she had fallen in love with. Just to be near him was enough. They sat close together on the deck, looking up at the dark, star-flecked sky. Then the others joined them for a while.

Someone was playing the victrola at the other side of the deck. Shirley Swayne was in the deck-house, playing backgammon with Josh. Winning lots of his money, probably . . . but Josh wouldn't care. . . .

A warm rush of sympathy for Josh . . . for the silly Evans sisters, for Evelyn Throckmarten who was going to marry the awful Browning boy, swept over Marjorie. She even felt a little sorry for Shirley Swayne . . . for everybody who wasn't going to marry Allie. . . .

Little pictures of her life in England—the kind of life Josh had described—formed in her mind. A big English home, with red-cheeked bobbing servants, and old, velvety green lawns, and rose gardens. . . . And she and Allie welcoming house parties—not like this one . . . nicer house parties. . . .

She hoped that Mid Bennett would come, and Erskine Gander. . . .

"Happy?" Allie asked.

She nodded, smiling a little.

His arm tightened around her. It hurt a little, and it wasn't comfortable, because the night was so warm. But she smiled, tried not to mind. She had better marry Allie and not make her mother unhappy. He was really very nice, and it would be fun, being Lady Fitz-Hamon—just as Josh had said.

Long after they had parted, she lay, wakeful and happy, in her cabin, glad that she had come.

# CHAPTER XIII

BUT next morning everything was wrong again. The houseboat was abeam the unprotected Florida Straits. A Caribbean swell was running and several of the party were ill. Mazie-Beth was in a vile humor, and she and Henry had had a scrap.

"I don't mind a rough sea in a ship that is built for it, but this barge should never have been brought into these waters."

"Let the skipper do the worrying, will you?" Allie asked tartly. "That's what he's paid for, you know."

Fortunately it didn't last long. They were soon back in the northern passageway, running in between low-lying coral reefs.

"At least it was cooler in the open sea," Mazie-Beth then complained. "And I don't like this kind of scenery myself. It's too creepy."

Mazie-Beth and Marjorie were about the only two who were interested in the scenery. The others, even the Evans girls and Shirley Swayne, had settled down to what promised to be a day devoted to serious drinking.

On the port side, from among dirty white porous reefs, hummocks of thick-trunked Royal Palms rose in clumps, from the twisted roots of mangrove jungle. Whiskery gray moss overhung the banks. Countless orchids, spotted brick red and greenish yellow, clung to the trees. A receding tide left millions of crawling things clinging to the snake-like roots of the mangroves. Scorpions with hard backs, some blue, some dark red, each with the characteristic cross on its back.

"Deadly poison," Mazie-Beth said. "Once I saw one in a bunch of bananas. But otherwise we don't have them in California."

"Well, the birds are lovely anyway," Marjorie added. Long-legged blue cranes stood knee deep in muddy water. Great pink flamingoes twisted sinuous spindly necks to watch the houseboat pass. Big beaked pelicans patiently fished in the shallows. Flocks of ducks, geese, swans and plover winged overhead.

"Oh, what's that funny bird? Get it for Mona! Mona wants it!" the giddiest Evans brat, clinging tight to Josh and Henry, danced up to the rail.

"Traffic policeman. You can tell by the bay-window," Josh explained, emphasizing his remark with a pinch.

"No! Mona wants to know birdie's name!"

"Pelican," Henry said. "But that is not the interesting thing. The interesting thing is the post upon which the bird is standing. It is a guidepost to navigation. It keeps us from running aground—that is, provided we stay within the signs. But as they are not lit at night we shall either have to use our searchlights, or cast anchor if we are still in the Keys—"

"Oh, shush!" Mazie-Beth begged. "The next man I marry is going to be illiterate, really. I'm so sick of being married to an encyclopedia."

"I should think you would welcome the opportunity to get something into your empty head," Henry said with dignity.

"Let's not quarrel," Josh put in heavily. "Let us, instead, return to the cup that cheers. Come, Henry—join us, girls?"

"No, thank you!" Mazie-Beth said tartly. And then turning to Marjorie. "You see what happens when you come on a party like this—they're drunk now, and they'll stay drunk until we get back—if we don't all get killed before that."

Henry, whose ears were good, wheeled and came

right back. "Are you—do I understand you to insinuate that I am drunk?"

"No—I'm *saying* you are; I'm not insinuating anything!"

"Then you are wrong, my dear. I am not drunk. Tight perhaps, but not drunk. A great difference, I assure you."

"Ooh, what are the funny men doing? Mona wants funny mans!"

"Shut up, Mona!"

"The funny men," said Henry, ever the gallant, "are sponge fishers. They dig down to the bottom with their poles, and bring up the sponges. They're alive, you know."

"Mona doesn't like them—Mona doesn't want any more sponges—doesn't want any animal 'ponges—an'm'l 'ponges."

"But they're sterilized—all the animal matter removed before you use them—"

"Oh, Henry—you *fool!*" Mazie-Beth cried.

Unexpectedly she burst into tears, ran weeping to her cabin. When Marjorie followed, hoping to comfort her, the door was locked.

"Anyway we can have lunch, even if Mazie-Beth is mad!" Henry, in his cups, rather liked the idea of a hungry Mazie-Beth.

"Let us drink, not eat," Josh voted.

"We can always do both," Marjorie said, but she recoiled from Josh's affectionate arm. He was so different from the Josh of yesterday. She felt lost without Mazie-Beth's moral support. "I'm the only sober person except Mazie-Beth on this whole boat . . . and she's locked in her room," she thought unhappily. "And they're all horrid except Allie . . . and Allie . . ." Well, Allie wasn't quite himself.

Filipino boys in immaculate white duck brought steaming clams, a huge salad, a macedoine of fruit.

Josh sat down next to the burgundy. Shirley Swayne, in emerald green lounging pajamas, ate nearly all the fruit. Nobody but Marjorie was hungry.

They were coming into Cæsar's Creek. In the ways lay Mrs. Arthur Curtis James' sumptuous yacht *Lanai,* patriarch of the Florida houseboat fleet. She was flying the coveted pennant of the New York Yacht Club.

A stone's throw away were Barron Collier's palatial steam yacht *Aera,* Tony Drexel's clipper bowed *Sayonora,* John Ringling's *Zalophus,* John J. Raskob's *Boksar,* Bill Leed's *Flying Fox,* and Percy Pyne's small fast cruiser *Brook the Second.*

Josh staggered out on deck to have a look at them. His bleary eye lit. "That," he said, buttonholing Henry, who was by now his bosom friend, "is Mr. Hannan's yacht *Comfort.*—Mr. Hannan makes his money in shoes. Buys comfortable yachts —haw, haw!"

"Haw, haw!" Henry echoed.

Marjorie did not smile. She was sick of them and their drunken jokes. She stood at the port rail, looking across the azure waters to the Cocoalobus Fishing Club, dwarfed by its tall white flagpole, flying the club's private signal.

Marjorie wandered around like a lost soul. She curled up in a deckchair with a book, but found she couldn't keep her mind on it.

Childishly she thought of the house parties that she had planned to have in England, at Allie's country place. If she'd have to worry always about his drinking too much, it wouldn't be very much fun.

Dressing for dinner took a little time, and gave her a little pleasure. She chose an eggshell handkerchief linen, with diminutive sleeves, and a long French blue ribbon sash.

Allie's moist hands left ugly marks on it, when he squeezed close to her at dinner, insisted on keeping one arm around her, lifting his glass with the other. He refused food, sang bawdy songs.

The Evans girls applauded wildly, joined in the choruses with gusto.

When Allie attempted to leave out some of the more ribald verses, Josh supplied them in a whiskey tenor. He knew thirty-seven verses for "Barnacle Bill the Sailor," and sang them all.

Then he began to tell dirty stories, prefacing each one with, "This is all right. This is really just a parlor story."

"Never mind, you're a big girl now," Allie whispered in Marjorie's ear, when she would have left the table.

Henry nodded in his chair. John Browning put his head on Evelyn Throckmarten's shoulder. They drank from one glass, passing it shakily from mouth to mouth.

The Evans girls bobbed up and down, doing Hula dances that nobody watched. Then Henry got up: "I've seen the natives in Samoa do one. You know—Samoa—the island—British possession. It goes like this—"

Amid shouts and applause Henry executed a few strange steps, sat down suddenly, rolled over, and fell fast asleep.

"Now, Shirley—you! You dance!"

Shirley Swayne lifted a languid, beautiful head and smiled slowly at Allie. "I wouldn't think of it."

"Please!"

"Atta girl!"

"Shirley!"

"Yes, please do!" Marjorie heard herself asking with the others.

Shirley Swayne, dragging rose and mauve chiffon draperies, rose slowly, went to the center of the cleared space on the deck. For a moment she smiled at the little group at the table. Then without preliminary, and without music, she pulled her skirts above her knees, did an old-fashioned music-hall gig, whistling her own accompaniment as she gigged.

It was over in a moment—a tiny, perfect thing, full of fire and mad, laughing rhythm.

Shirley dropped the chiffon skirts suddenly, trailed back to the table, sat on Allie's lap. "That's my baby!" Josh complained. He got up heavily, padded around to Allie's chair. "Come to Papa!"

Shirley put her long, graceful arms around his neck, permitted herself to be carried away to Josh's corner.

"Flora used to do that sort of thing," Allie shouted across to Shirley. "Did it damn well too!"

Flora. . . . Marjorie knew that was Allie's first wife.

"Yes? Why did you leave her then? She was a cute trick," Shirley drawled.

"I didn't—she left me!"

"No woman ever left you—no woman ever will, Allie!"

Marjorie winced, hoped she wasn't going to be ill. What were they thinking of? Didn't they realize how embarrassing this was for her?

"Left me when the family froze her out!" Allie chuckled. "Wasn't my fault! I told her what they'd do. But she would go to England. Deuced hard on me, too. Wouldn't get any reception if I came alone, but with an ex-chorus girl . . ." He chuckled again. "There was Flora, with five trunks, a maid and two Pekes, prepared to move right in. My aunts—mean old girls—asked her to sit down and have tea. They had their hats on—as if they were going out some place.

" 'I hope you will have tea with us again sometime,' my Aunt Sophronia Isabella says.

" 'Yes, do call again,' murmurs my aunt Victoria Marie—and Flora's trunks on the drive—and the

Pekes yapping. . . . God, it was *my* most embarrassing moment. But what could *I* do?"

Above the shouts of drunken laughter Allie began again: "Should have seen us wandering around the gardens before we went in. Me pointing out the flowers. All the holly bushes, and the hawthorns, and the—well all the flowers. Trying to get up nerve to go in, do y' see? And Flora yelling, 'What's the idea? I didn't come to look at flowers. I want to get in. What the hell's the idea?' . . . Very—very funny."

"Here, here!" Josh bawled.

"Here, here!" The others took up the cry, kept it up.

No one bothered to eat any more. Dinner, somewhere in the middle, seemed to be over. Giggling Filipinos removed the remains of the feast.

Marjorie rose and attempted to go to her cabin. Like Mazie-Beth, she had had enough of the party.

Allie was right at her heels.

"Don't go, darling—don't go leave me! Sit on my lap. You haven't ever sat on my lap. . . . Don't you love your Allie? Good God! I hope you're not going to turn out one of these cold American women. Don't pull off that way. . . . Kiss me. . . . Hold still. . . . I never saw such a girl. No—don't push me—I'll lose my temper. I'm not used to being knocked around. Thank you!"

Marjorie pulled away—gave him a final shove that nearly floored him.

"Allie, you're drunk. You're disgusting!" she sobbed.

"Never you mind. . . . I may be drunk, but I'm a gentleman. I'm not a nouveau-riche, spoiled child. No need for you to get on your high horse. You can jolly well get off of it now. I've treated you like a Sèvres vase for six weeks, and I'm damn tired of it. I'm serious too—I'm not going to put up with you. Do you hear me? Now, kiss me—kiss me, I say! . . . Oh God! If you'd only learn a thing or two from Shirley—"

The last was a drunken wail, perhaps not meant for Marjorie's ears, but she heard—slapped him with all her hard young strength. He reeled against the wall, clung to a chair for support.

Marjorie covered her face with her hands. "I've hit him," she moaned, "I've hit him, and he's drunk. . . . Oh, I can't stand it! Why did I come? Why did I?"

Allie had recovered his balance. "Yes, why did you? You've done nothing but queer the party since you came."

With a muffled sob, she turned, almost ran into the closed door of the deckhouse, then downstairs to her cabin. The door slammed behind her.

In an agony of fear and shame she threw herself on her bed and cried her heart out.

Hours later she rose to listen . . . the sounds of revelry continued. Above the blare of the phonograph she heard Allie's song, and Shirley Swayne's voice. . . . "Whooopee!"

## CHAPTER XIV

THE Havana Limited was steaming out of New York, Florida bound. Among its wealthy and distinguished passengers was Vincent Duke of New York.

In the club car he met his old friend George Canfield, bound for ten days' racing at Miami.

"I'm just going to Palm Beach to get my daughter, Marjorie," Duke said. "She's been there for the past six or eight weeks, and I think she's getting homesick for her dad. She was on the point of announcing her engagement to an English peer wintering down there—you know the ideas young girls get. I think she has changed her mind, though. She's got a good head. Quite a lot like me, in many ways. I believe she's changed her mind. Quite a blow to her mother if she has. Alice, poor woman, has set her heart on a title!"

Canfield smiled understandingly. He, too, had a wife.

At Jacksonville a short thickset man in a gray suit boarded the train. He walked with the flat-footed shuffle peculiar to ex-policemen.

He was, in fact, an ex-dick. Federal Inspector Fred McNulty of Chicago.

Depositing his bag, he went directly to the observation car, and tapped at compartment C.

"I'd like to see Mr. Vincent Duke, please."

"Mr. Duke is napping. I can't disturb him," Ward Robinson, Vincent's elderly secretary, replied.

McNulty pulled back his coat, displayed the familiar badge. "I'm afraid I'll have to trouble him."

Robinson shook his head, as he walked over to the communicating door, and entered the drawing-room A. It had been a hot, tiresome trip, and he didn't anticipate a very cordial reception from his chief.

Duke sat up and mopped his forehead. "Well, show him in. Guess it's about the jewels. Let's get it over with!"

McNulty took off his derby, held it stiffly. "Terrible hot country for a Chicago boy in the heart of winter. But I've got something very important to tell you, sir."

Duke motioned him to a seat. "Make it as brief as possible. I'm trying to get a little rest on this trip."

"It concerns your daughter."

"My daughter! You're crazy."

"Isn't it your daughter who is engaged to marry Allan Fitz-Hamon?"

"The engagement has not been announced. I can tell you more about that after I've seen my wife."

"At any rate he's violated the United States Narcotic Act."

"Preposterous! You have the wrong man!"

"No, sir. I have his picture right here. The Illinois authorities have already telegraphed instructions for his arrest. I'm going to bring him back with me."

Vincent Duke stared at his visitor for a long moment. "This is an amazing story," he said at last. "But I may as well tell you that he and my daughter are not engaged. They have never had my consent, and I believe the girl had already changed her mind. You'll see that she's kept out of any trouble in connection? You'll keep her name out?"

McNulty looked sympathetic. "I know just how you feel, sir. I'm a father myself. You'll have to see the newspaper men about that. But I'm sure you can fix it."

"God, I hope so. Have a cigar?"

McNulty smelt it, lit it hopefully. "Well, I can

count on your support in helping locate the fellow."

"Certainly. Don't go—sit down and tell me about it. How about a cold drink?"

"Thanks. Mind if I take off my coat?"

"By all means. Make yourself comfortable. Comfortable as you can on these trains. What's this Fitz-Hamon mixed up in? Dope, did you say? He takes dope? He's a hop head? My God, I thought at least he was respectable."

McNulty settled himself, braced his feet on the seat opposite. "Oh, he's respectable. That's how he got in the racket. You see there's a lot of opium smuggling going on on the East Coast. These fellows figure that there isn't much chance on the Pacific Coast any more. It's too well watched. So their racket is to buy in the usual markets in the Orient and India, ship the stuff to Europe, and then back to the East Coast here. We've been watching West Palm Beach and Miami, and we're just about ready to close in on them."

"Humm," said Vincent Duke.

"There are a lot of big shots in the racket—a lot of big names—men you'd think were pretty upright business men in Wall Street."

"Business men, eh?" Mr. Duke coughed slightly.

"Yes, sir. There's always a master mind at the head of one of these rings, some racketeer who's been in for years. Then he hires high sounding names—you know, men who can go anywhere and put up a good front. Sometimes it's a young fellow who's gone through all his old man's money and wants to clean up and start all over again. Right now they've got a lot of washed up Wall Street bulls and bears, or whatever you call them fellows.

"Well, this Fitz-Hamon"—McNulty was warming to his story—"was one of the high-grade men. Everybody knows this Lord Allan fellow, and he looked good, see? He could go to a fence—acting on his boss's instructions, see?—and nobody think anything of it. He wouldn't be watched.

"Say, he'd be sitting pretty to-day if a little fellow the police picked up in Chicago on a gem robbery charge hadn't got sore and squealed on him."

"I see," Mr. Duke murmured vaguely. The day was moist, and he did not follow all of McNulty's terms. He thought, "I must draw the fellow out. This is terrible. Marj might have married him. She would have if she hadn't listened to her old dad's advice. . . ."—"Go on—I'm all attention."

"Well, it seems that this little fellow, Dutch Louie, they call him, is the one who lifted your daughter's diamonds . . . by the way, did the insurance company pay full value?"

Vincent Duke bit into his own cigar violently. "Not yet."

"No? Better get a lawyer. You got to watch those fellows. Crawl out every time if they can . . . what was I saying? Oh, yes—Dutch Louie. . . . Well, sir, this Dutch Louie was mixed up in the same dope business, in a small way. We had the goods on him, and after a little manœuvring we got him to turn state's evidence, and once he started, that little fellow told plenty.

"Why, he gave us names and addresses that would turn your hair gray. Lots of them were women. That's quite a story in itself. You see, these girls in the choruses of some of the big musical reviews get the idea they want to be stars and they sell out to some old bird with dough. You know how that is. When the old bird is through it's either go on down the line, or back to the chorus. One thing leads to another, and first thing they know they're in with a pretty hard lot. Blackmail, dope peddling and worse. Now, sir—that is where you'd be interested in the names—"

"Yes?" Vincent Duke was only human. He leaned forward.

McNulty waved a plump hand. "I can't disclose the names, though, of course. But they're all high class people, with money enough to pay these girls plenty to keep their mouths shut. The revenue runs into hundreds of thousands—the girls work on a percentage basis—do you see?"

Mr. Duke saw. But he wanted to hear more about the man who had come so near to being his son-in-law.

"I hope this Dutch Louie fellow doesn't revive that necklace story again. I don't want my daughter's name dragged into the papers. What else do you know about Fitz-Hamon? Never liked the fellow—what I knew of him—myself."

McNulty accepted another cigar. "Oh, he wasn't such a bad egg. Funny thing though. . . . It seems that Dutch Louie's wife, Ivy Brown—used to be in the Scandals, fine-looking big blond—liked this Fitz-Hamon pretty well. Fitz-Hamon has quite a way with the women, they say.

"Well, sir, this griped poor little Dutch Louie. It seems he was also sore because Fitz-Hamon wouldn't help him out on any little deals he was pulling, like this jewel business where they made the big haul at the Gibbons party. Fitz-Hamon could have given a lot of assistance and he wouldn't do it. Old Louie got sorer and sorer thinking about it, because he figured Fitz-Hamon could have saved him from getting caught—so he gave it all away, and Mr. Lord Allan Fitz-Hamon is going to be the most surprised gentleman in Palm Beach when he gets the news."

"He's out on a houseboat with my daughter and a big party, I'm afraid," Mr. Duke said.

He was really worried. Marjorie at sea with that cad . . . this ugly scandal breaking. He rose to shake hands with his informer, gave what little information he had on the houseboat, promised to keep in touch with him at Palm Beach.

Just as the train pulled into the station, a breathless, hatless young man swung onto the rear car and elbowed his way through a line of disembarking passengers, into the drawing room of Vincent Duke.

"I'm Gander, *New York Sketch*."

Mr. Duke recoiled as if he had been stung.

"And I'm looking for a Mr. McNulty. I understand he was in here with you, sir!"

"I suppose your paper is all primed with the news," Duke said dryly.

"Oh, yes. I've been getting it over the telephone; we're all ready to spring it. It may be on the street in New York by now."

Again Mr. Duke recoiled. "I trust my connection with the case is not mentioned?"

"You mean Miss Duke's? Oh no, sir. Trust me to—"

"You're keeping her name out? What?"

"Oh, yes. Marjorie's a friend of mine. What I want to do is to get—"

Vincent Duke's arm was entwined in that of the breathless young newspaper man.

"Have you any influence with these other newspaper boys?"

"Been drunk with most of them, sir!"

"Get them to keep Marjorie's name out!"

"I'll do my best!"

"The Breakers!" Duke told his secretary. "Get a cab and take care of the bags, will you? I want to have a few words with this young man. I'll be along later."

## CHAPTER XV

TWO men put out in a skiff from the Cocoa-lobus Fishing Club, made their way to the *Nautilus,* swinging at anchor on a rising tide.

Five minutes later the ruddy-faced little captain went to Allan Fitz-Hamon's cabin. Allie, fully dressed except for his shoes, lay on his bed where the Filipino boys had carried him. He was sleeping heavily, his handsome face flushed, clothes wrinkled. The room reeked of gin and stale cigarette smoke.

The fastidious Key West skipper wrinkled his nose with disgust. Gingerly he shook the sleeping man. At first mutters and groans were his only response. Finally Allie opened heavy eyes. "What the hell is the matter?"

"Something serious I'm afraid, sir."

Allie pulled himself to a sitting position. "Yes, something serious would happen—after last night. Well, out with it. Has the engine blown up, or did some fool set fire to his bed?"

"Nothing like that, sir. It's a message they just

sent over from the Club. All radio stations are asking for the location of the *Nautilus*. Any craft knowing our whereabouts is to notify the Customs at Palm Beach or Miami at once. We're instructed to put in at the nearest port immediately."

There was a moment's silence.

"Pour me a shot—a stiff one. Got to clear my head," Allie said at last.

The skipper poured.

Allie downed the stiff drink at a gulp. He stared at the little skipper speculatively. "What do you make of it?"

"Must be something about the liquor, sir."

Allie groaned. "That will place me in a fine spot with Colonel Roget."

"Colonel Roget is always very careful."

"Yes—and I wasn't. But what the hell could I do with a load of booze-hounds like this?"

"Shall I start back at daybreak, sir?"

"What about the fishing? How do I know that radio isn't some nitwit's idea of a joke?"

"It's no joke, Lord Fitz-Hamon. Radio stations don't joke with the Federal authorities."

Fitz-Hamon began ripping off his wrinkled clothes. "I'm going to have a cold shower. I'll let you have my decision afterwards."

The little captain looked embarrassed. "I'm sorry, sir. As Colonel Roget's skipper, and representing his interests, I have no alternative. We'll have to start back with the first light."

"Very well," Fitz-Hamon answered lightly. "I simply wonder that you went to the trouble of notifying me, since my opinion is of no consequence."

The man's embarrassment mollified him somewhat. "At least do me the kindness of letting me explain to my guests, will you?"

The skipper saluted awkwardly, backed out of the stuffy cabin. For a moment Allie sank back on the edge of the bed, covered his aching head with his hands.

Then he made his way to the shower.

An hour later, in the first light of the new day, the *Nautilus* had weighed anchor, was heading back in the direction whence she had come.

Stewards were washing down the decks, removing the mute evidence of last night's drinking orgy. Empty bottles went splashing into the pale green waters, sticky glasses were carried back to the galley and scoured.

Presently the deck, at least, was shipshape. Allie Fitz-Hamon, heavy-eyed, but immaculate in white flannels and sweater, sat at the charmingly set breakfast table and consumed his solitary meal, while his drinking companions of the night before slept below.

Once more he was the perfect gentleman, debonair, poised, attractive.

What thoughts were going on behind that expressionless, well-bred mask of his face no one could guess.

While he sipped black coffee, nibbled dry toast, ugly fear settled soggily into his numbed, tired brain. Half-formed plans scuttled across his consciousness. There was no longer any doubt in his mind about the significance of the message. What to do? He couldn't decide. . . . If only his brain were clearer. . . .

There he sat, lost in his cold, ugly fears. . . .

Fingers toyed with toast, automatically lifted the coffee cup. Eyes, expressionless and pleasantly clear under their heavy lids, followed the glittering, molten ball of the sun as it rose above the green water, reddened the eastern sky. . . .

On New York streets newsboys were shouting, "Uxtry! Uxtry!" Rushing from early riser to early riser, glaring headlines held aloft:

PALM BEACH SMART SET
IN DOPE EXPOSE

Scion of Ancient English Nobility Faces
Second U. S. Prison Term

Business men, with papers propped on the breakfast table before them, let three minute eggs grow cold while they read Erskine Gander's really excellent story of the United States' brilliant work in uncovering a gigantic, far-reaching scheme for bringing opium in its various nefarious forms into Atlantic seaboard ports.

Shopgirls, hanging to straps in subway and elevated, read over lurching shoulders.

Maids, placing neatly folded papers on breakfast trays, took a second look at handsome Lord Allan Fitz-Hamon, then the insert of him in convict stripes—alias Bert Allan. . . .

For Goose's hunch had been right after all. He *had* seen Lord Allie in stripes. It had been back in the days when San Quentin—that bleak gray prison on California's windy San Francisco Bay—had prescribed stripes for its inmates.

Goose was a cub reporter on the San Francisco *Herald* then. He had gone to San Quentin for a field day the prisoners were having.

In that sea of faces, one had stood out, the face of a thin, aristocratic young Englishman, with fair hair, clear eyes, thin, sensitive mouth.

Goose didn't know who the man was. He had no interest in finding out.

Yet six years later it came back to him, but his years of newspaper work had taken him to too many jails, too many penitentiaries. He could not remember where he had seen it.

It remained for the Hall of Records, supplied with the thumb prints and photographs Goose had pinched from the Gibbons' ball, to trace it.

Goose felt a little sorry for Allie when he heard the pathetic, sordid story from his managing editor, over the long-distance wire.

The Fitz-Hamons, it seems, had all but washed their hands of Allie. They expected a certain amount of nonsense from a high-spirited, spoiled lad like him. They had paid, out of their scanty funds, for two wrecked Isottas, a biplane, and a music hall girl's broken heart. They had put up with more than they thought necessary. They had given more than they could afford.

So after the affair of the biplane, and a heavy damage suit from the owner, they shipped Allie to Canada with a thousand pounds a year, and the earnest advice that he behave himself.

He hadn't. To avoid certain difficulties with a more or less respectable married woman in Toronto, he had gone, first to Vancouver, then to Seattle. In Seattle he had worked in a lumber mill for ten days, then beat his way to San Francisco.

With seven and a half in American money in his pockets he had taken rooms at the St. Francis, and waited for something to turn up.

When the money was gone, and Jimmy McCabe had made it plain that a check would have to be forthcoming, he had left his bags behind him, and moved to a rooming house in South San Francisco.

There he registered as Bert Allan. He was having one of his periodical attacks of conscience. He decided to begin work in some humble way, become a captain of industry, and amass an American fortune. He was, at the time, very young, you see.

The only work that was forthcoming was dishwashing. Allie washed dishes for four hours. Then he put on his hat, and left.

A chance acquaintance from the St. Francis hotel lent him twenty dollars. With it Allie purchased a second-hand suitcase, of respectable mien, and registered at a better boarding place.

He had written to his aunts for money, and expected it any day, but in the meanwhile he couldn't starve. He thought of borrowing from a Captain Fanshaw, a Toronto sportsman, visiting in town. Captain Fanshaw was out. So, not without trepidation, Allie wrote a check, signed Fanshaw's name. It was cashed without question.

Emboldened, he repeated the performance elsewhere. If worse came to worst, he could, he thought, explain that he, Bert Allan, was really Lord Allan Fitz-Hamon, temporarily out of funds, but good for the amount, of course. To his very great surprise Captain Fanshaw prosecuted. Allie was all too glad to stick to his playful alias, and serve time under that name.

When he emerged from San Quentin he was both sadder and wiser. He had had time to reflect upon the ways of a naughty world, and to hold converse with gentlemen proficient in the art of living without working.

The next six months witnessed the come-back of Lord Allan Fitz-Hamon. He was seen frequently in the company of middle-aged women whose wealthy husbands did not understand them. His name figured prominently in the society columns.

Flora Fulton of the Follies (born Leona Hauch) spent a quarter of a million of an elderly Dallas millionaire's money on him and then decided to marry him.

After that failed, he drifted again. His connection with the narcotic ring had always been rather casual. At least he carried on his dealings in a casual manner. Goose shrewdly suspected that he had never admitted, even to himself, that he was really a cog, and an important, highly paid cog, in the machinery of turning opium into dollars. It remained for the Federal authorities, and little Dutch Louie Broune, to decide differently.

As Inspector McNulty said, Allie wasn't a bad egg—comparatively speaking. The world is full of comparative eggs.

Goose, generous in victory, tried to put that idea over to his managing editor. Fortunately for him, the connection was poor. George Clark didn't hear more than half of what his star reporter was saying.

And now the fat was in the fire. The facts were out, and Inspector McNulty, like a great gray spider, waited patiently for Fitz-Hamon's capture.

Goose—usually calm in the midst of excitement—was feverish with impatience and anxiety.

"What's the matter with you? Quit hopping around. Are you in love?" Benny Lomond, his successor on the *Press,* demanded. Lomond was looking for Palm Beach news fit to print.

Goose was really in a jam. His work would suffer if he left Palm Beach. He'd probably get canned again. But Marjorie's father had asked him to go along on the Coast Guard speed boat, which was even now getting ready to put to sea after the *Nautilus.* He couldn't give up that chance. Marjorie would probably hate him for his part in the mess, but he had to go, he had to be in at the finish. . . .

"Be ready in twenty minutes, will you, Gander?" Vincent Duke telephoned.

"Sure, meet you on the dock."

Goose hung up the receiver, remained leaning against the door of the telephone booth. . . . Maybe Benny Lomond would cover Rum Runners' Row for him. . . .

And then he had one of his better ideas. He'd ask Helen Ilderton . . . give her that chance she'd been waiting for. . . . And with Benny to look after her, show her the ropes, and do most of the work she'd be all right. She could at least file the wires, see that some sort of yarn got in every day. . . .

He called her number.

"Helen! Great news. . . . I've got a job for you. . . . No, it isn't exactly a job; it's batting for me for a couple of days. . . . Get all the society gossip on bootlegging you can. . . . Yes, I know you've got a lot.—Fine!—And make Benny Lomond read it before you file it—Benny will tell you how to do it. I'm going to tell him now. Remind him of all the favors you did for him when you were with Gibbons.—Thanks a lot, Helen! It will be swell experience for you.—No, I can't talk any more—got to run. Big story.—No, I'll be out of town for a couple of days.—'Bye!"

Goose looked at the watch on his wrist. Risked another precious three minutes talking a reluctant Benny Lomond into showing Helen Ilderton the ropes.

"I don't mind helping you out," Benny said. "But why pick that skyscraper? You might have given me a break with some cute kid."

"Go on, Benny—be a sport—please!"

Goose couldn't risk another moment. He left it there. Dashed out of the hotel, hailed a taxi.

"Drive like hell!" he bellowed.

They reached the dock just as the narrow gray Coast Guard launch was pulling out.

One of the newspaper men on board saw the familiar, hatless figure tearing down the wharf. Vincent Duke interceded for him. They went into reverse.

Breathless, grinning, too winded to speak, Goose waved his thanks. Then they were under way.

## CHAPTER XVI

ABOUT seven o'clock Marjorie Duke emerged from her cabin, came out on the deck. She had cried most of the night; her eyes were still somewhat swollen and red. Her delicately featured little face was pathetically young and pinched. The heat made the dark hair cling to her forehead in damp curls. In her straight blue linen frock and flat heeled white shoes she looked like a little girl.

Worry and disillusionment had not robbed her of her appetite. She ventured on deck because she was hungry. The smell of coffee and bacon had drawn her out.

It was nice to be out in the air again. She stood by the rail for a moment, drinking in the salty air. Then she rounded the deckhouse and found Allie, still sitting at the breakfast table, having his third cup of coffee, his sixteenth cigarette.

She drew back, startled. "I—I didn't think you'd be up yet," she said, and turned to leave.

Allie was on his feet. "Won't you please have breakfast, Marjorie—and let me apologize for last night?"

She reddened, shrank back, her hands behind her.

"Please don't make me feel any worse than I do already," he begged.

She saw that he was in deadly earnest, that he, too, looked ill, and his eyes were strained, as if he had not slept. So she came forward slowly, and dropped into the chair opposite him.

"It's a lovely morning, isn't it?" she asked. She was afraid she'd scream, or burst into tears if she had to sit facing him, and he just looking at her tragically, saying nothing.

"Marjorie," he said slowly, "I can never tell you how much I regret last night. I have in my lifetime done many things that I am ashamed of, but nothing . . . no, nothing . . . that I regret so much."

"It's quite all right. Let's not talk about it—please, Allie."

A Filipino boy brought grapefruit, a mound of golden scrambled eggs. Toast, steaming coffee. A silver bowl of guava jelly, and a plate of Cuban cheese.

Marjorie secretly regretted that she wasn't more like girls in books . . . unable to bear the sight of food after a heartbreaking affair like that of last night.

But here she was, helping herself to more

scrambled eggs, with her life ruined, and her ex-fiancé tragically eyeing her across the breakfast table.

After another uncomfortable silence Allie began to speak again, "You realize, of course, that I was not myself? That I had been drinking?"

"Oh, yes!"

"That as the host I—I'm not inventing extenuating circumstances—had to drink with the guests?"

Marjorie's lip curled ever so slightly. "I understand."

"Then, Marjorie—could you forgive me?"

"Yes, Allie. I forgive you."

Allie's heavy eyes rested doubtfully, then hopefully, on Marjorie. . . . A half formed plan began to take shape in his mind. . . . God! A wedding at sea . . . and the Dukes' fifteen millions between him and the pen. . . . If she'd do it . . . and why wouldn't she? Never lose your nerve . . . nerve is what gets a man through worse than this. . . . He leaned forward. "Marjorie," he began earnestly.

"Hello, early birds!" It was Mazie-Beth, bright-eyed, freshly tubbed, immaculate in white shantung. "Allie too! For goodness' sake! I'm surprised. Judging from the noises I heard last night I thought all the males on board were as drunk as Henry, and here's Allie fresh as a daisy. . . . Oh, guava jelly! I love it—no, don't get up, Allie, just bring another chair.

"Isn't it a grand morning? Just like Catalina. Has anybody seen Henry? I locked him out of the cabin. I suppose he had to sleep with the sailors!"

Allie, with a mumbled excuse, wandered away.

"Such a trip," Mazie-Beth sighed. "You don't know how I have suffered. I thought at least you'd come to see if I wanted anything."

"Wanted anything! I nearly broke down your door trying to get in!"

"Marjorie! When?"

"When you first went down."

"Oh—then. I didn't mean then. I meant later. I had the awfulest time trying to call a steward without letting Henry in. He wanted to get in, in the worst way—on account of his pipe—but I wouldn't let him."

One by one the others appeared. First the Evans girls, giggling and asking for ice water. Then Evelyn Throckmarten, sullen and quarrelsome in orchid negligée and ostrich-tipped mules.

John Browning was the last to appear.

The beautiful Shirley refused to get up at all. She slept all day. . . .

Josh and Henry Lawrence, arm in arm, both decidedly the worse for wear, staggered on deck shortly after Evelyn arrived, but declined breakfast with cries of horror.

"This is a fine lot," Mazie-Beth said disgustedly. "I thought you were all going fishing. I thought that was why we came out here."

"Allie says the fishing is no good in Cæsar's Creek; we're going to Jewfish."

The Evans girls began to giggle.

"That's the name of another Key," Henry explained.

"Dlink! Dlink!" Josh bellowed. "How do you ask for a drink in Filipino, Henry?"

"Oh, they speak English. Here, boy!" Henry called.

The thirsty ones reached for the glasses on the Filipino boy's tray. "Hoopa Doopa," he explained. "Some other one plain tomato juice, goo' for next morning."

"Well, I'll have a Hoopa Doopa," Josh said. "It smells like it might have gin in it."

Marjorie began to count the hours until their return. Not that the return would be a particularly happy one. There'd be a scene with her mother. . . .

Poor Marjorie's knees felt weak when she thought of that. How could she face it? Her mother would weep, and she would probably be ill. . . . The shock might even kill her.

The papers, too. They'd all have something about it, and the scandal sheets would be vicious. . . . People would point her out . . . a girl who almost married a title, and then didn't. . . .

There would be the rest of the season to get through in New York—for her mother wouldn't stay in Palm Beach after this. . . . And next season she'd have to be an old girl, a left-over, and watch the season's debs. . . .

Maybe nobody would marry her, and she'd go on for years and years, looking older and older, and acting gayer and gayer, and finally marrying some nobody who'd be vulgar and make a great splash with Father's money. . . .

And all because she got started wrong. . . .

Or maybe it was because she was too squeamish. Maybe other girls wouldn't mind the things that Allie had done. . . .

She hunted up Mazie-Beth. "Mazie-Beth, do you

think it's very awful if a girl doesn't marry in her first season?"

"I think it's awful if a girl marries at all. I wish to goodness I had stayed single. I'd be home with my Mother right this minute. Henry just makes me *furious*. He—"

But Marjorie couldn't talk about Henry. Her own troubles pressed too heavily. "I mean—if I don't marry this season, will it be hard for me next season?"

Mazie-Beth considered. "Mm. . . . I suppose it will, a little. If you're going to get married you might as well do it this year, and have it over with. They're all alike anyway. . . . Hen! . . . Hen! I want you. . . . Run down to the cabin, will you, like a nice boy, and get me my panama hat?"

He came back with the hat, and his own fishing tackle. "I've never tried my hand at deep sea trolling. I believe I'll have a go at it. They're bringing the fish boats alongside."

"I don't know why you want to go. You know you don't eat fish," Mazie-Beth said.

"I'm glad the boats are going to be used, anyway," Marjorie smiled. "It would have been too bad to tow them all the way from Palm Beach and then not use them."

Henry and Mazie-Beth went off to see about the fishing. Marjorie looked after them wistfully. She knew that the girls would be expected to remain on the houseboat, but she would have liked to go. At least it would be something to do.

Allie and the little skipper were engaged in earnest conversation in the deckhouse. Some sort of argument, evidently.

Presently Allie left the wheelhouse, went and stood for a moment looking moodily out to sea. . . . Was it a pose?

Unaccountably Marjorie's heart began to plunge. She was afraid! Something was going to happen . . . trouble. . . .

At that moment Allie turned, met her wide, frightened eyes.

"Is something wrong?" he asked, hurrying to her.

"No—nothing. I don't know why I— Just a funny feeling. It's nothing, Allie."

He stared at her earnestly, as if he were trying to read her thoughts. "Funny. . . . Are you sure you're not clairvoyant?"

"Allie, of course not!"

"My thoughts were very troubled, Marjorie. Shall I tell you what has happened? I've kept it from the others. I thought I wouldn't worry them until I had to. Shall I tell you?"

"Yes—I won't do anything foolish, Allie."

He looked at her for a moment with genuine admiration. "You're a thoroughbred. . . . I hate to tell you this, Marjorie. It's rather a mess, I'm afraid. Last night the Federal authorities put out a call for us. We're wanted. When we land I'll be put under arrest—perhaps all of you—I don't know."

"But why? I don't understand, Allie—I don't see—"

"Neither do I, exactly. The skipper believes that it is on account of our failure to observe the twelve mile limit law. While we were still at the pier, Henry and Josh, and one or two of the others, were on deck with bottles. My fault, of course. It places me in a most embarrassing position. Not only do I ask my friends out for a little fishing, and land them more or less in jail, but I'm in a horrible spot with Colonel Roget. He lent me the boat. I don't know what they do about those things . . . confiscate it, perhaps. . . . Good God, I've nothing—how will I pay for it?"

"I don't know."

"Marjorie, you said you'd forgive me."

"Yes—I have."

"Marj—this seems such a caddish thing to ask of you, but I'm in such desperate straits, and if you've forgiven me they're your concern as well as mine. . . . Marjorie, would you marry me—now—let the skipper officiate?"

She gulped, found no word—just stared at him, her blue eyes hurt and troubled.

"Does you out of a wedding, and all that, doesn't it? It's a thing no man should ask of a girl, Marjorie. . . . It is taking a mean advantage. . . . I wouldn't ask it, if there was any way out. But it will save so much trouble, for you, as well as for me."

"Why?"

"God, I feel like such a rotter, having to tell you this. But it's on account of your father's position, darling. As Vincent Duke's son-in-law, I'm solvent. . . . I can get out of it some way. I can square things with Colonel Roget. It will even take the curse off it for the others on board. They'll be so excited over the wedding, they'll hardly notice the other thing, do you see? Same with the damned newspaper men. . . . They'll crowd down like ghouls to get the news on the one thing, and they'll go away with snaps of you and me posed together at the rail—and maybe the skipper marrying us

. . . the happy end! Grand finale—everything fine. . . . Do you see?"

Marjorie had not taken her wide eyes from his. "Yes—I see, Allie."

"Marjorie! Darling—I knew you would—I knew!" His arms were around her, trying to hold her tenderly. "Oh, my love, what can I say to you? Except how happy we'll be later—how—"

"No," Marjorie answered wearily, "don't hold me, Allie, please. It just makes it harder for me. I—I did love you once, Allie. That's why it has all hurt so . . . why it hurts so much to let you down now. But I won't marry you, Allie. I just couldn't . . . not after what you've just said."

Allie stuck his hands in his pockets. Began to speak very quickly, as if his moments for argument were to be but few. "Marjorie, I'm not altogether insensitive. I know that your—your love has gone—for a time at least. I have only myself to thank for that. . . . But there's more than love to be thought of in a marriage that unites a name as old as mine, and a fortune as great as yours. Perhaps we were wrong to have even expected love, Marjorie."

He watched her, and she nodded, as if in agreement. He went on, still speaking swiftly. "You would have the age-old title, Marjorie—and I'd—well, I'd have some—" Then he stopped. "It sounds very cold, doesn't it?"

"You are being very frank, Allie."

"I don't think it would be purely a business proposition. I think we would be very happy, Marjorie."

"No, Allie. No—it's too late."

"Then, my dear, even if we weren't happy . . . so few achieve happiness, Marjorie. There would be the other things—the peace, the security of England, my decent family—"

"No, Allie. No!"

For a long moment Allan Fitz-Hamon gazed into Marjorie Duke's eyes.

Then, without another word, he turned on his heel, and went below to his cabin.

The youngest Evans girl was jumping up and down. "Mona wants fishie! Mona wants fishie!"

"Sorry, but I can't accommodate you," young Browning said coolly. "I for one am not going. I don't care for deep sea fishing. There are no gamey deep sea fish. All that interests me is barbless dry fly-fishing in mountain streams."

Josh Huntington held a gin fizz midway between table and mouth. "How about a sail fish? Not game enough for you?"

"No, and I don't believe the stories about their towing boats a hundred miles, and I don't believe the one about their standing on their tails to fight, either."

"How about the trout story? The one about the pet that fell overboard and drowned? Could you believe that?" Josh inquired.

"I have fished in Restigouche, Campbell River, the Stampp—in fact all over the world."

"Have you tried worms in the Rapidan? Cal Coolidge and Herbie Hoover do fine work with worms, I hear."

"That isn't game fishing, Mr. Huntington!"

"Damn fine eating!"

"I never eat fish. The whole thing is sport with me. I have hundreds of different kinds of flies."

"Ever try Flit?" one of the Evans girls giggled.

"I keep my flies in specially made aluminum cases, each fly in its own glassed-in partition."

"When he's Henry's age," Mazie-Beth whispered, "he'll be worse. Imagine! I didn't think it possible!"

"I'm sorry. If you're going to fish you had best start," Allie said. He had changed into khaki, and in the brown costume he looked old and tired. "The Captain wants the fishing boats to keep ahead of the *Nautilus*. I'm sorry, too, but owing to an unavoidable change of plans there will be no opportunity for real deep sea fishing. We must proceed straight ahead. . . . Sorry. Does anyone mind very much?"

"All right with me," Josh said.

"Same here," from Henry.

Sailors had drawn the fishing boats, which had been towed at the stern, around to the starboard side. Henry and Josh climbed in one with a sailor.

"Come on, Allie! Plenty of room!" Josh, who had almost fallen overboard getting in, was now comfortably seated in one of the swivel wicker-chairs.

"No, thanks. No fun fishing with a crowd—I prefer to go alone."

"But you can't go alone. It isn't safe!"

"Safe enough, Josh! I'll swap fish stories with you later," Allie laughed. "Bet I catch more than you do!"

The first boat was gathering speed.

Allie jumped into the second, raced the engine, forged ahead.

The little crowd of women on the *Nautilus* waved. Allie waved back, then disappeared from sight.

## CHAPTER XVII

THE U. S. Coast Guard cutter *Dolphin* sped through the pale green waters of the Gulf Stream, made its circuitous slow way through the winding ways in the Keys.

Some of the newspaper men were a little nervous.

"We ought to anchor inside, and wait for morning," somebody said.

"I heard one of the Coast Guard men say the lighthouses are displaying hurricane warnings," another said. "Small boats are told to keep in."

"We're a small boat, aren't we?"

Vincent Duke listened dispassionately. His was a one-track mind. He had come for the purpose of finding Marjorie, bringing her back. He had no interest in his own personal safety.

But he was tired—very tired. The scene with Alice hadn't added to his peace of mind. She had made a fuss—an ugly fuss. Not that he minded that so much. He was too used to Alice and her tantrums to be much disturbed by them. But this was something more serious.

Alice was ill. Not make-believe illness either. He recognized the lines of real suffering on her thin, grayish face. Alice's health was all right; the family physician had repeatedly assured him of that. So if she had worried herself into such a state, things must have come to a pretty pass between her and Marjorie.

He suspected her of forcing Marjorie to go on the trip. Marjorie had said plainly in her letter that she didn't want to go. Vincent Duke lit a fresh cigar, took a puff, and let it go out while he stared moodily out to sea. He blamed himself for not coming sooner. He had delayed for a directors' meeting. To save a few paltry thousands he had perhaps imperilled his daughter. "I'll retire. . . . I'll go traveling with her," he thought, "I'll take her away somewhere where she can forget all this, and Alice can come, or not, just as she pleases."

And then he caught a remark someone near him was making. "A steel boat like this will stand anything."

Steel. . . . What about his Consolidated shares? He should have wired the home office.

There he was, thinking about business . . . couldn't keep his mind off of it. . . . Just a rotten habit—bad as the dope habit. It chained one so.

Impulsively he took the arm of the young newspaperman he had taken such a fancy to. "Young man, are you too young to take advice?"

Erskine Gander grinned. "Don't think so. Why?"

"Never let business get too great a hold on you, my boy. Never get the money-making habit. It will rob you of everything that's worth while in life."

Goose laughed out loud. "I wish you knew my managing editor. He's the one that needs that advice. I guess my trouble is that I don't let business get a big enough hold on me. I'm always getting fired."

"Drink?"

"No, sir. That is, not very much. Not enough to get fired for it."

"Women?"

Goose laughed again. "Not the way you mean it. But I get soft-hearted about the widows and orphans—keep stuff out of the paper for the sake of some swell-looking girl or other."

Vincent Duke regarded him steadily. "Hmm," he said, at length.

After another pause. "I once knew a man named

Gander. Thomas Erskine Gander. Lumbering man in the Northwest. Any relation?"

"He's my dad, sir," Goose's throat swelled.

Again Vincent Duke regarded the young man steadily for some moments. "Hmm," he commented, at last. "You his son? Well!"

It had been another long, difficult day on board the *Nautilus*.

Everyone was tired, hot, and out of sorts. Everyone was sick of dancing, sick of shuffle-board, sick of drinking, sick of making love, sick even of quarreling.

They sat around in deck chairs, dozed with magazines open on their laps.

"I wish Henry hadn't gone," Mazie-Beth said at intervals. "He has a very weak stomach, and if they catch any fish it's sure to make him sick. It's too sultry to catch fish down here. Henry's used to trout fishing in the redwoods. My, I'll be glad when we land."

Shirley Swayne, in pajamas, gave her a withering look. "We'll all be glad when we land.—I never found Hollywood half as interesting as Broadway, my dear. Too many fish and the Southern California pool's too small."

The little skipper was in the deckhouse, busy with binoculars. Sailors hurried back and forth. There was an air of suppressed, unhappy excitement, of something closely akin to foreboding, hanging over the once merry party.

"It's hurricane weather," John Browning said. "I know the signs. We're in for it. You can see the captain is worried. I wouldn't like to be in one of those little fish boats when it breaks."

"Surely you don't think we're in danger now?" Shirley Swayne sat up, her tanned face paling. "If there were danger wouldn't he tell us?"

"Tell us? I thought you were an experienced ocean traveler? Why, they never tell the passengers. They don't want a panic."

"Why don't they call in the fish boats?" Evelyn asked. "I should think that would be the first thing a skipper would do!"

"Who do you think we've been tooting for, the flying-fish?"

Mazie-Beth covered her face. "Henry! Out there in that boat! Oh, why did he go? I told him not to! Oh, I wish we'd never come." She began to sob hysterically.

"And what of Allan Fitz-Hamon, all alone?"

Shirley asked disdainfully. "Or is your husband the only one who is in danger?"

"Oh, I don't want anything to happen to my Henry," Mazie-Beth sobbed. "I'll regret it so—I've been so m-mean to him. Oh, I'm so worried!"

"Mazie-Beth, dear, don't worry—I'm sure it's all right," Marjorie tried to comfort her. "I've often heard that there are no hurricanes here except in the late fall—and then way out to sea. I'm sure Henry's in no danger."

"Oh, you don't understand. My life would be just ruined without Henry! You just don't know how I feel."

With a groan and a mumbled: "Can't endure any more of that woman," Shirley Swayne retired to her cabin.

"Please, Mazie-Beth, don't cry so."

"Josh and the sailor and Allie are in danger, too, you know," the oldest Evans girl said, "and Marjorie is being brave. She isn't crying!"

Marjorie turned a sudden, startled face to her. They'd expect her to be anxious about Allie. Well, she was, of course . . . about them all. But Allie . . . how could she tell them?

"Here they come!" Brownie announced. "I knew they'd respond to the signals. Wonder if they caught any fish." He was standing at the rail, his binoculars focused on a dark spot way ahead.

"Here they come! It's Josh and Henry."

"And Allie—any sign of Allie?"

"No, just the one boat."

They waited, a tight little group at the rail, while the fast fishing boat came back to them.

Josh Huntington, red-faced and triumphant, stood in the bow. "I caught an amberjack," he shouted. "So heavy he almost capsized the boat. All Henry got was a Portuguese man-of-war!"

"I was just getting a bite," Henry called to the crowd on the deck, "when we had to turn back. It was a kingfish—I distinctly saw it."

Mazie-Beth was holding out her arms. "Hen! Hen!"

"Did you hear me, Mazie-Beth? A kingfish—I almost caught it."

"Kingfish! When I've sat here, crying my eyes out on your account. Oh—I might have known! Oh—what's the use!"

With a stifled shriek Mazie-Beth covered her face with her hands, ran crying to her cabin.

So when Henry, hot, tired, and dirty arrived at the door he found he was locked out.

"Go away!" she sobbed through the door. "Go away!"

"I don't know why a kingfish should upset her so," Henry told Marjorie. "Did I say anything else that could hurt her feelings?—Say, don't give Fitz-Hamon a reception like that when he turns up. Ruin your prospects. I wish I were a bachelor. I do indeed!"

Marjorie smiled wanly. "Without intending to be, you're very comforting, Henry, for I've decided to be an old maid—for the present at least."

"You're off of Allie? Why, Marjorie, I'm surprised. I thought you such turtledoves."

She saw him cast a troubled eye in the direction of Shirley Swayne's cabin. "No, it isn't for any particular reason," she said frankly. "Just everything. But it's all over. You can tell Mazie-Beth if you like."

"If she ever lets me in."

Marjorie almost smiled as she heard him beating on the cabin door a little later. Perhaps it was just as well that she wasn't going to get married. . . .

Allie's boat hadn't come back.

The skipper had Henry and Josh in the deck-house, quizzing them.

"The sailor tells me he went through the inlet to the Gulf Stream. He thought he was after something more gamey out there.. Did you see him return?"

"No," Josh said. "I hooked the amberjack right away and I was too busy with him to think about Allie. He's an experienced fisherman, you know. He's fished all these waters. He'll take care of himself."

"I'm trying to find out where he went," the skipper said irritably. "I shall have to send out for him in the other boat."

"Tut-tut—he's a man and he's just chasing something—sailfish maybe. Why, I've heard of sailfish taking a man—"

"And you, sir," the skipper cut in, addressing Henry, "did you make any note of Lord Fitz-Hamon's direction?"

"He made off for the open water—that's all I noticed."

"Thank you, gentlemen—that's all."

Scarcely thirty minutes later the *Nautilus* sighted the searchlight of another boat.

"There he is!"—"There he comes!"—"Good old Allie!"—"Bet he's made a haul!"

Henry Lawrence shook his head. "No—that's

not the fish boat. It's a much larger craft—coming awfully fast!"

As usual, Henry was right. . . . Princeton makes men like that.

It wasn't Allie and the lost fish boat. It was the U. S. Cutter *Dolphin* speeding to them.

The skipper was very grave. He came out of his quarters in the deckhouse, and called the little group of guests to him.

"In the absence of your host, Lord Fitz-Hamon, I feel that it is my duty to explain something to you," he said. "United States Coast Guard officers are approaching. In view of the fact that we were instructed to put into the nearest port, by radio last night, I believe I am right in concluding that an investigation of some sort is pending. I ask your coöperation in answering any questions that may be put to you. Thank you."

They stood in a close little group, silent at first, then a babble of whispers, questions, a stifled giggle or two from the Evans girls, a murmur of indignation from Shirley, a frightened cry from Mazie-Beth.

The cutter was close alongside now. Sailors were throwing the rope ladder over the side. The light from the *Nautilus* illumined the deck of the other boat. Half a dozen men in civilian clothes, pushed close behind the uniformed Coast Guard officers, waited their turn to come over the side.

For a second the ray of light fell on the upturned face of a hatless, freckled young man, with windblown, fair hair.

Marjorie Duke leaned over the rail of the *Nautilus*. It was . . . no, it wouldn't be . . . it was just someone that looked like him. . . .

She pushed Mona Evans aside unceremoniously —almost trod on the toes of a boarding revenue officer, stumbled over a cushion someone had left on deck.

The fair young man was at the rail now. He threw one leg over, leaped to the deck.

"Goose!" Marjorie cried. "Goose! It's—it's you!"

"Marj!"

"Oh, Goose, it's been terrible. I—I can't tell you—" She clung to him—put her dark curly head down on his shoulder.

Automatically Goose's arms tightened around her.

"Oh, I'm so glad you came. I—I just couldn't have stood anything more. I couldn't—I couldn't!"

"Marj, honey—listen. Your—"

"Oh, Goose, take me away with you on that boat. I want to go home."

"Marj—listen—your—"

The expression on Erskine Gander's face, as he soothed the sobbing girl he loved, and felt her wet little face so close to his, was not of unmixed bliss.

The girl's father was just behind him, and a New York millionaire who has had a long, hot trip to rescue his beautiful daughter from an impecunious peer can hardly be expected to be pleased at finding her in the arms of a penniless newspaper man.

"Listen, Marj," he began again, this time more firmly. "Your father's here. He's right here—look up, honey girl—right here."

Marjorie gulped—lifted her tear-streaked face incredulously. Still clinging to Goose's arms, she looked around her.

"Marjorie, dear, you're looking right at me!"

"Father! Father, I'm crying so I didn't see you. Oh, you came! You got my letter and you came!"

She had gone from Goose's arms to her father's. He was stroking her hair.

"I should have come sooner," Vincent Duke murmured. "I won't ever forgive myself. You'd have been saved all this."

The newspaper man stood for an awkward minute or two, watching the reunited father and daughter. Then, with a funny little wry smile he turned on his heel. "Get the hell out, will you, Goose?" he said to himself. "Can't you see you're fired?"

Pushing past the crowd, with the impersonal efficiency of his kind, he elbowed his way to the front rank in the wheelhouse where the investigation was going on.

It didn't take him long to gather what had happened. Allie had made a getaway, or a try for it anyway.

"What chance has he to make Nassau, sir?" he asked the perspiring skipper.

"I should say about one in ten."

One in ten. Goose considered. It was like Allie Fitz-Hamon to do that. To take the long chance rather than face the certainty of arrest, and probable conviction for violation of the narcotic act. He rather admired Allie. "Hope he makes it, damned if I don't," he told the man from the *Eagle*.

"Yeah? Makes a better story for us. They'll be scouring the Everglades for him for weeks."

"No, I don't mean it that way. I admire the nerve of him."

The Coast Guard boat was preparing to begin the search for the missing Allie. Guests, knowing half the truth, gossiped in twos and threes.

"I'm not the least surprised. He was always queer in some ways."

"I didn't want to come on this party anyway. Just did it because I couldn't get out of it."

"Tough on Colonel Roget."

"Tough on all of us. We'll all be dragged into the papers.."

Mazie-Beth Lawrence, with solemn-eyed Henry at her heels, came over to greet Vincent Duke.

"It was very lucky you came," she said, "and I hope that you bring Marjorie right out West where men are men. Marjorie isn't the type for this fast life. I've lived in California all my life, and I've never, never been in such a humiliating situation as this!"

Shirley Swayne, in traveling clothes, traveling case in hand, as though she were going to disembark in a moment, drew Marjorie aside.

"I congratulate you, my dear."

"I'm afraid I don't understand. Why are you congratulating me?"

Shirley Swayne smiled. "On your luck in not having announced your engagement. Now that poor Allie is in disgrace you can deny it so beautifully. You can say you never were engaged. So fortunate."

"I never was officially!" Marjorie answered hotly. "And I broke it off last night anyway—principally on your account. So if you wish to congratulate me, I'm sure I should thank you!"

"Really—" Shirley began.

Fortunately for Marjorie, Josh Huntington heaved in sight, and averted what might have been an unpleasant scene by bellowing, "Put your bag down, Vicomtesse, we aren't landing just yet. We've got a good six hours to go!"

Shirley turned away with a shrug of distaste.

"That woman has been a total loss ever since she got on board," Josh said. "That's what comes of thinking you're too good for common, ordinary mortals. She used to be a real nice girl when she waited on table in Henry's in Hollywood. Soon as she got to be a star she went sour, and since she married the Vicomte—whew!"

Marjorie smiled wearily. "I think I'd better get back to Father, Josh. I left him talking to Mazie-Beth."

"Just one minute. I want to show you this." In his hand Josh held an Eastern paper one of the newspaper men had given him. With clumsy tact he had it folded to hide the pictures of Allie, but he pointed a thick finger at the rather blurred cut of a piggy-eyed little man over the caption, "Dutch Louie tells all."

"What did I tell you? That's the guy I said took my pile at Bradley's. Same one bumped into me at the Puritan. Damn rum runner, that's what he is. . . . Where's Goose? I'm going to give him a scoop. Hey! Goose! What did I tell you about the fellow who took my pile at Bradley's? Didn't I say he was a crook? Look—same face—couldn't ever forget it. I told Ivy—"

Goose grinned. "But Ivy is Mrs. Dutch Louie. You couldn't blame her for sticking up for her husband, Josh!"

Even Marjorie smiled at Josh's chagrin.

"Hell!" he said. "I never thought of that!"

"Didn't you know it? It's been in the papers for days."

"How should I know it? I've been too busy fishing!"

They all laughed, and then Goose led Marjorie aside. "Your father wants to see you a moment. We're going to have to leave you. The Coast Guard is going to put back to Miami for instructions, and we've got to go with him. They'll search for Fitz-Hamon's boat on the way, and you'll probably go on back to Palm Beach. . . ."

Marjorie's face fell. "Oh, no—don't go. Stay with us. Or let me go back with you. That would be better. Please do, Goose! With you and Father—"

"But I don't think they'll stand for it," Goose was saying as Vincent Duke came up. "I'll go and see though."

Marjorie repeated her plea to her father. He shook his head. "No, I wouldn't ask it, my dear. It would make too much trouble. You must remember that all of these people want to land just as much as you do. It wouldn't be very sporting for you to ask."

"All right," she answered, as bravely as she could, "but you don't know how I'll feel, seeing you and Goose go away."

"Sorry, Marjorie, it can't be done," Goose said, coming back after a brief conference with one of the Coast Guard officers. "But perhaps you can persuade your father to stay with you on the *Nautilus*."

"You too, Goose! You both stay—please!"

"I'm afraid I should get back to your mother. I

was a little worried about her. You stay with her, Gander."

Marjorie looked up at Goose expectantly, her heart in her eyes.

Goose looked down at his shoes, grinned slowly. Marjorie wanted him to stay and if it would make the poor kid any happier. . . . But damn it, if he did that he'd miss out on any news about Fitz-Hamon, and he'd be canned again sure. . . . Just one more flop for him. . . .

He raised his eyes. He was going to explain. But Marjorie! Damn the job! "Sure, I'll stay with you, Marj. I'm not invited, but it isn't the first time I went to a party uninvited, is it?"

"No! That awful dinner at the Everglades Club—will you ever forget it? It was when we really started to be friends, wasn't it?"

"All aboard!" a sailor shouted from the *Dolphin*.

Vincent Duke made a movement toward the ladder. Marjorie tore her eyes away from Goose's. " 'Bye, Father—you're a dear!"

He kissed her gently. "Good-bye, Marjorie girl. I'm leaving you in good hands. You'll be all right."

Goose stuck his hands in his pockets, still grinning sheepishly.

"Never mind about losing that job. You don't

want to work for a cheap yellow paper like the Sketch," Duke was saying. "Come on back to New York with me, and I'll fix you up—get you a real job."

"Oh, Goose! Father means it! He never jokes about things like that! Isn't it wonderful? I'm going back to New York too!"

That settled it.

"I just financed your dad's bond issue," Mr. Duke was saying.

"Fine! I'll come!" he shouted across to the *Dolphin* where his future employer was standing with a group of sailors and newspaper men.

"All right. Maybe I'll make you old man Gander's junior partner!"

The newspaper men guffawed. Everybody but Marjorie laughed. She blushed, and turned her pink, happy face away from the crowd.

If Father said that, he meant it, and if he was going to do that . . .

Goose turned to her, grinning. He was happy. He was going to have some hours alone with Marjorie. Maybe he could make her take him a little more seriously. Maybe she'd even . . . well . . . maybe she'd consider him real seriously, if he were off the yellow paper, and settled down in a decent business with his dad. . . . This was going to be fun, and in New York where he could see Marjorie often. . . .

Marjorie's thoughts were way ahead of that. She was planning how she'd dress her bridesmaids . . . in autumn colors, pale yellow to burnt orange, and maybe she'd wear gold instead of white, though after all, there was nothing quite like white. . . .

"Good-by, Marjorie! See you soon!" her father shouted from the departing *Dolphin.*

She kissed her hands to him. " 'Bye, dear! Tell Mother not to worry. . . . Father—explain—everything to her. Please!"